D IS FOR DRAMA

ALSO BY JO WHITTEMORE

Front Page Face-Off

Odd Girl In

D IS FOR DRAMA

JO WHITTEMORE

aladdin m!x
ALADDIN M!X
New York London Toronto Sydney New Delhi

ALADDIN M!X
Simon & Schuster Children's Publishing Division
1230 Avenue of the Americas, New York, NY 10020
First Aladdin M!X edition August 2012

For information about special discounts for bulk purchases, please contact
Simon & Schuster Special Sales at 1-866-506-1949 or business@simonandschuster.com.
The Simon & Schuster Speakers Bureau can bring authors to your live event.
For more information or to book an event contact the Simon & Schuster Speakers Bureau at
1-866-248-3049 or visit our website at www.simonspeakers.com.
Designed by Hilary Zarycky
The text of this book was set in Berkeley Old Style.
Manufactured in the United States of America 0712 OFF
2 4 6 8 10 9 7 5 3 1
Library of Congress Control Number 2012938568
ISBN 978-1-4424-4152-1
ISBN 978-1-4424-4153-8 (eBook)

To my high school drama teachers,

who ALWAYS made me feel like a star

ACKNOWLEDGMENTS

Always for God, family, and friends.

And for: my fabulous editor, Alyson Heller; my ever-supportive agent, Jenn Laughran; my irreplaceable critique partner, Cheryl Peevyhouse; and the Steeping Room teahouse staff, who put up with me every week and are as sweet as their desserts.

But especially for those who said "Go for it!" and talked me through it when I said I wanted to write a humorous book dealing with discrimination: Jessica Lee Anderson; Matt de la Peña; Bethany Hegedus; Kari Holt; Ellen Hopkins; Tricia Hoover; Varian Johnson; Jeanette Larson; Cynthia and Greg Leitich Smith; Cynthea Liu; April Lurie; Linda Sue Park; Cindy Pon; Michael Reisman; Don Tate; and Emma Virjan—you guys (and gals) rock my world!

ONE

THERE ARE A NUMBER OF horrible ways to die at Carnegie Arts Academy. You could be crushed by a piece of falling scenery, strangled with piano wire, even kicked in the throat by an angry ballerina.

But the worst way to go would be under the daily stampede in the halls. To survive at CAA, you have to follow the crowd . . . literally.

When a swarm is on the move, it's either to reach something good (free ice cream in the caf) or to escape something bad (Jill Hudson practicing opera scales). You can usually guess the reason based on who's leading the charge, but there's always a voice in the crowd who shouts it for all to hear.

On the second Monday of January, mine was that voice.

"Play results are up!" I cried. "Know your fame or know your shame!"

The principal, who was leading a tour, pushed his group aside right before they were trampled.

"And *those* would be the ambitious students in our theater department," he said, sounding annoyed.

I wasn't sure why. We'd skipped the sparklers this year, and his new wig looked *way* nicer than the old one. It was probably less flammable, too.

Plus, we had a good reason to be excited!

Every semester, CAA's theater department put on a major performance, and every spring, it was produced by the graduating class of eighth graders. This spring, the show was an updated version of *Mary Poppins* called *Mary Pops In*. And since there weren't a lot of female parts, I was beyond nervous.

CAA followed the unwritten rule of all drama departments since the dawn of time: Any theater production should star the same three or four kids each year. Always. Unless one of them dies.

Sadly, that never happened, so I remained a bit player, tackling such gripping roles as Girl in Crowd or Villager Number Three. One semester, I didn't even make it onstage. I just shouted from behind a curtain for background noise.

My parents were *so* proud.

In my defense, it wasn't that I lacked talent. Nobody at the academy had a louder voice, according to my teachers, and my best friend, Chase, assured me I was plenty dramatic. Not to mention, my mom had been a famous actress in Korean cinema. Theater was in my blood.

Yet *my* name, Sunny Kim, always fell somewhere on the bottom of the casting sheet. And when the playbill came out, I was listed under Extras, like an unpopular topping on a sundae menu.

I was the shredded coconut of the theater world.

So why was I excited about audition results this time? For starters, my friend Ilana was on the selection committee. She thought I was a good actress *and* she would keep things fair . . . unlike last year's committee.

(I burped *once* during a death scene. Like nobody has gas at a funeral.)

But this year, besides having Ilana on my side, my acting coach, Stefan, said I'd nailed my audition. It was just a matter of finding out which starring role was mine.

I sprinted toward the theater with students tussling and shoving behind me, and more joined the stampede, including Bree Hill. She and I grinned at each other, and Bree shouted something to me.

I couldn't hear her, partly because of the crowd, but mostly because of Bree's soft voice. Her shouting isn't much louder than the squeak a hamster makes when you accidentally tap-dance on it.

But Bree doesn't need volume to be a great actress. She has poise and confidence and a way of really stepping into character. I know because she and I have been audition buddies since we started at CAA. And like me, she never gets the big parts.

I leaned closer, and she shouted again.

"I'm so excited!" she said. "I'd love to be Mary Poppins . . . or even Jane Banks!" She raised her pinky and I hooked it with mine.

"I know!" I shouted back. "As long as I don't end up in the potato sack, I'll take any speaking role!"

The potato sack wasn't a theater term. It was *literally* a potato sack that had been my costume as Villager Number Three. While the main cast wore professionally tailored costumes, the ones for bit players were cheap, homemade, and badly sewn.

Bree smiled sympathetically. "You'll get something *great*. Suresh and I both think you rocked the auditions." Suresh was Bree's boyfriend and another member of the theater crowd. He always wound up with slightly better parts since he was a natural at dance numbers, but he still wasn't a Chosen One.

"Thanks," I told Bree. "Maybe lucky audition five will be the winner!"

Instead of answering she squeezed my arm and pointed at the bulletin board outside the auditorium. A sheet of yellow paper was pinned to the cork . . . a sheet that hadn't been there Friday.

Bree and I both dashed forward. The other students pressed up behind us as everyone struggled to find their names on the top of the list.

"Mary Poppins, Mary Poppins, Mary Poppins," Bree chanted over and over. Her finger settled on the name, but before I could see what was written beside it, a tall, red-headed guy stepped in my line of sight.

"Chase!" I bent from side to side, trying to see around him.

"Hey! What part did you get?" he asked.

"I don't know." I pushed him aside. "Bree! What's it say?"

Bree turned to look back at me, her expression one of sheer disappointment. "Sunny, you—"

I didn't need her to finish that sentence. The look on her face, the "S" I could clearly see her pointing at . . . I gasped and dug my nails into my cheeks.

I was Mary Poppins!

My excited shriek sounded far and wide, much to the annoyance of the kid standing beside me. With an apologetic smile, I reached for my cell phone to snap a pic of the casting sheet. Photo number one in my dust-covered album of success!

"Sunny?" Bree tapped me on the shoulder.

I shooed her away while I pulled up the camera feature on my phone. "Pay attention, people!" I bellowed to the crowd. "Something amazing has happened!"

"You've learned violence isn't the answer?" asked Chase.

I punched him and held my phone up to the bulletin board, trying to pick the best angle for my victory photo.

"Sunny . . ." Bree tugged on my arm.

"Oh! Take my picture!" I thrust the phone at her and stood against the wall, reaching up to point at Mary Poppins. "I want to . . . uh . . ."

I paused and leaned back to study the board. Now that I was closer, something seemed off. "Wait," I said, frowning. "Sunny isn't spelled S-a-r-a."

I turned to Bree, whose crushed expression had returned.

"That's what I was trying to tell you," she said, her voice quieter than usual. "Neither of us got it."

"Oh," I said. The joy that had been bubbling inside me was rapidly cooling to a sludge of shame. "Well, maybe . . ."

I searched the board for my name, hoping, praying for something almost as good. But I wasn't Jane Banks. Or Mrs. Banks. Or Mr. Banks. The sludge in my stomach thickened to a hard lump. My eyes scanned down, down, *down* the list and finally spotted my name at the bottom.

Sunny Kim . . . Villager Number Two.

I stared at the bulletin board, willing it to rearrange the letters into something else. Or to explode into a billion pieces.

Even with a friend on the selection committee, I couldn't get better than an extra. Was I really that bad?

Chase bumped against me. "All right! Villager Number Two!"

I gave him a pained expression. "I thought I was Mary!"

His forehead wrinkled. "Married? I guess you could be *Mrs.* Villager Number Two."

I stared at him. "*Mary!* As in Mary Poppins?"

"Ohhh." Chase's confused expression turned into a frown. "I'm sorry, Sunny." He put an arm around me.

"Thanks," I said. "What part did *you* get?"

Chase stiffened. "Nothing."

"What?"

"No one," he tried again, stepping away. "Definitely not the male lead."

I rolled my eyes and glanced at the casting sheet. He was Bert the Chimney Sweep, Mary Poppins's quasi-boyfriend.

Of course.

Chase *was* one of the Chosen Ones, partly because of his talent and partly because of his scruffy red hair and green eyes. He was pretty cute, and girls willingly forked over allowance to see "pretty cute."

"Awww, think of it this way." He put an arm around my shoulder. "At least you're not Villager Number *Three*!"

I took his face in my hands and smiled sweetly at him. "Hold very still. I'm going to headbutt you."

"Not his nose," murmured Bree, who was still staring at the bulletin board. "That's our moneymaker."

Chase pulled my hands away. "All I'm saying is that this role is an improvement."

"But I wanted a *lead*!" I groaned in annoyance and joined Bree. "This is so lame." I flicked the casting sheet with my fingers. "Sara doesn't even *like* being onstage. And the first time she tries out, *she* gets the spotlight?"

"Maybe she has natural talent," said Bree.

I shook my head. "Remember when she read *Macbeth*

in class? I thought Shakespeare was going to dig himself up and smack her with the shovel."

"I don't think Shakespeare was buried with a shovel," said Chase.

"My point," I said, giving him a look, "is that the casting is always wrong and always unfair. I'm Villager Number Two, Bree's the . . ." I looked closer at the sheet.

"Village whisperer," she supplied.

"You see?!" I threw my hands in the air. "And we're not the only ones in ridiculous roles." I rattled off names as I scanned the rest of the audition results. "Suresh is a backup dancing chimney sweep, Anne Marie's the pigeon lady in the park, Wendy Baker's Villager Number One . . ." I paused. "How come she gets to be Number One?"

"I think because she's actually British," said Bree.

I frowned. "But she doesn't even *like* tea."

"Focus, Sunny," said Chase, eyeing the clock on the wall. "I've got five minutes before baseball practice."

CAA didn't have an athletics program, but Chase's dad wanted him to have a "sensible hobby" to balance "this acting nonsense." So Chase pitched for an intramural baseball team. He wasn't bad, either.

"Right," I said. "My point is that the starring roles in

the spring production are never about talent; they're about who you know."

"Thanks," said Chase.

I grabbed his arm. "I didn't mean you. You have *plenty* of talent. Someday, they're going to rename the auditorium after you."

"That's enough," he said.

"I thought the whole point of Ilana being on the selection committee was to keep things fair," said Bree.

I snapped my fingers. "And that's why I'm talking to Ms. Elliott. She may not be running *this* production, but as the drama coach, she should know what's up, right?"

Bree and Chase exchanged a look.

"What?" I asked.

Chase put his arm back around my shoulder and steered me in the opposite direction of Ms. Elliott's office. "Sunny . . . we've been friends a long time, right?" he asked.

I nodded. "Ten years. Since you moved in down the street."

"Right." Chase smiled. "And in ten years, I've seen the look in your eyes *right now* a dozen times."

"What look?" I asked, standing a little taller. "Grim determination? Unfailing courage?"

"Insane madness," he said.

"Hey!" I ducked out from under his arm.

"It's the same look you had at seven when you tried to jump off your roof in a cape," said Chase.

I studied my reflection in a window. "There's no madness in these eyes."

"*And* last year when you asked the caf to stop serving fish so your hair wouldn't smell," he continued.

I crossed my arms. "The cute guy from my math class said I reeked like tuna."

"He was a jerk," said Chase. "You smell nice. You always have."

I blinked in surprise. "Really?"

Chase blushed. "My point is that you look like you're about to charge off and do something dumb. Don't."

Clearly, Chase didn't understand the gravity of the situation. I was meant to follow in my mom's theatrical footsteps. *Success* flowed through my veins, not the mediocrity of being The Eternal Extra.

"I *have* to take care of this," I said. "I can't go back to my parents with another bit part. And what if I'm not auditioning correctly? I need to know."

"I thought you paid that high school guy Steven to help with that," said Chase.

"*Stefan*," I corrected him. "He changed his name when he got back from Paris."

Chase didn't look impressed. I placed a palm on his chest and pushed.

"*Go*," I said. "If you're late, your dad's going to flip and lose the last patch of hair on his head."

Chase grabbed my hand. "Just promise you won't make things worse."

I snorted. "Yeah, it'd be tragic if I lost this part."

Chase continued to stare at me.

"I promise," I said.

I shooed him away and turned back toward Ms. Elliott's office, almost colliding with Bree.

"I'm coming with you," she said.

"I *don't* need supervision."

"Actually," she said with an apologetic smile, "I'm coming to ask Ms. Elliott about *my* part."

"Oh," I said, leading the way. "Then let's go find out why we're not famous."

TWO

DESPITE MY PROMISE TO CHASE, my plan was still to storm into Ms. Elliott's office, but when Bree and I approached the door, we heard two people shouting.

In Shakespeare-speak.

"Why will you suffer her to flout me thus?" cried Ms. Elliott. "Let me come to her!"

A second voice that sounded a lot like Ilana's responded, "Get you gone, you dwarf! You minimus, of hindering knot-grass made!"

I glanced at Bree, who shrugged, and we both poked our heads in the doorway.

Ms. Elliott was reciting Shakespeare from her desk with

her eyes closed so Ilana could line them in kohl pencil. Ilana's long, brown hair was tucked under a baseball cap, and her gaze flitted from the script she was reading to her handiwork.

"Hello?" I called.

Ms. Elliott's eyes flew open, and she pushed away from the desk, giving an embarrassed cough. Ilana turned to us and smirked.

"Makeover?" she asked, waggling the eyeliner.

Ilana was always strapped for cash, and this was her latest money-making scheme. Every day, she strolled the halls with her cosmetic case, offering to turn girls into glamazons for the low, low price of ten bucks a sitting.

"You're getting *teachers* to pay you now?" I asked.

Ilana shook her head. "Just practicing. Business has been slow since the 'natural look' came back"—she scowled—"so I'm adding stage makeup to my skills."

Ms. Elliott nodded and held up a mirror to study the progress. "I'm auditioning for the city theater's *A Midsummer Night's Dream*," she said. "And Ilana's helping me with lines."

"Yep. Since I'm not in *Mary Pops In*, I have *loads* of spare time," muttered Ilana. She flung the kohl pencil in her cosmetic case with more force than necessary.

I knew why. Ilana was a Chosen One like Chase, and

she loved to act. In fact, she'd been accepted into STARS, an exclusive summer theater program. But here at school, the selection committee wasn't allowed into the spring production; they could only be understudies or crew.

"What can I do for you girls?" Ms. Elliott smiled at us while Ilana brushed rouge across her cheeks.

Bree stepped closer. "We wanted to talk in private—"

"Why didn't you give me a better part?" I asked Ilana.

"But . . . uh . . . thought we'd blurt it out instead," finished Bree with an embarrassed smile.

Ms. Elliott frowned and waved the makeup brush out of her face. "What's this about now?" she asked.

Ilana raised a halting hand. "I'll take care of it. You keep practicing your lines."

Ms. Elliott thought for a moment, then nodded. "I suppose it is a student production," she said. "Let me know if you need anything."

Ilana nodded and smiled at us again, pointing at the hallway. "Let's talk outside."

As soon as she'd shut the door, Ilana turned to me with her lower lip pouted.

"I'm *so* sorry!" she said in a whisper. "You were brilliant and I wanted you as Mary Poppins, but the others on the committee wanted Sara."

Ilana's confession momentarily stunned me. It was sweet that she'd suggested me for the role (and nice to know I *wasn't* a complete failure), but I couldn't help feeling disappointed that nobody else saw it that way.

"Why didn't I at least get a better part than usual?" I asked.

She smiled. "You did! Villager Number Two."

I clenched my teeth and took a calming breath. "I meant bigger than that. There has to be someone who—"

Ilana put a hand on my shoulder. "Sunny, the parts have been cast. I can't change the list."

"Sure you can," I said. "I'll even retype it for you."

She raised her eyebrow. "Do you really think that's fair?"

"No," I said with a sigh. "I guess not."

Bree cleared her throat. "If you can't do anything for Sunny, then what about me?"

Ilana tilted her head sympathetically. "Sorry, Bree. My answer's the same." She gave Bree a quick once-over. "But I can fit you in for a brow pluck tomorrow."

Bree covered them protectively. "I'm good."

Ilana nodded. "Then I should probably get inside. Ms. Elliott's makeup won't do itself!"

After blowing us kisses she slipped back into the office, and Bree and I stared at the closed door.

"So, that's it?" asked Bree. "She insults my facial hair, and it's over?"

"Not for me." I shook my head. "I'm going to be in that spotlight, one way or another. Wait and see."

When I walked home that afternoon, I was surprised to find Chase *not* at baseball practice but waiting at our usual spot, the massive oak tree on our street corner. He was tossing a foil-wrapped lump in the air and catching it behind his back. On one of his higher tosses, I snatched the bundle away.

"Lightning-fast reflexes!" I said. Then I tripped over a tree root.

Chase tried not to laugh as he offered me a hand up. "Maybe you should be a tumbler instead of an actress," he said.

"I would if the unitards were cuter . . . and not called unitards," I said, smoothing my hair and skirt. "What are you doing here?"

"Nice to see you too," he said. "Practice was canceled after the coach threw up in the dugout."

I looked down at the foil package in my hand. "I *really* hope this isn't a souvenir."

Chase laughed. "Of course not!"

Then he peeled back the foil so I could see the delicious pastry inside. My best friend was the only person I knew who preferred the bottom half of bakery muffins and always saved the tops for me.

I inhaled deeply and closed my eyes with a dreamy sigh. "Chocolate Monkey." My favorite flavor: banana nut with chocolate chips.

Chase leaned against the oak. "I thought you could use it."

"You are so, so wise." I took a huge bite of muffin, drawing comfort from the moist, cakey goodness.

Maybe Villager Number Two could eat Chocolate Monkeys as part of the character. Then I might not mind having such a lame part. Especially if I could pelt Mary Poppins with the chocolate chips.

"How'd the talk with Ms. Elliott go?" asked Chase.

"Perfect," I said, taking a big swallow of muffin. "She got me a job in Hollywood doing a movie with Jaden Smith. I don't even need Mary Poppins anymore."

"Oh, good," said Chase. "Then I *didn't* miss your mental breakdown."

"Ha ha." I kicked at the tree. "Ms. Elliott's too wrapped up in her personal life to help, and Ilana told me I didn't get the part because some other people voted against me."

Chase wrinkled his forehead. "I thought you were good. Are you sure?"

"That's what Ilana said." I buried my face in the aluminum foil and scarfed more Monkey. When I came up for air, I mumbled, "The whole thing's rigged."

Chase stared at me, looking pensive. "What are you going to tell your parents?"

"What *can* I tell them? I didn't get the part," I said, picking the last crumbs out of the foil.

Chase shook his head. "You can't just blurt it like that, though. You've gotta put spin on it."

I snorted. "Wonder where you got *that* from."

Chase's dad was a smooth-talking politician, and his speeches were filled with vague statements that people could interpret dozens of ways.

"I'm serious," said Chase. "You need to break the news in a different way."

I thought a moment. "How about—'Mom, Dad, once again I've embarrassed the family.'"

Chase rolled his eyes. "A different, *positive* way."

"Hey, Mom and Dad, you know how you were worried about *success* going to my head? I've got great news!" I threw in a thumbs-up.

"Maybe less sarcasm?" suggested Chase.

"I can't." I balled up the foil and tossed it to him. "My bitterness is too fresh." Setting my backpack under the tree, I dropped down to lean against it. Chase joined me.

"Maybe they'll forget about the auditions," he said. "Isn't your dad in the middle of a project?"

Dad composed music for film scores. That was how my parents met, while he was working on the sound track for one of Mom's movies.

I snorted. "Sure, but there's no way my *mom* would forget. She's probably been massaging her tear ducts to get ready for disappointment."

Chase bumped my shoulder with his. "Don't be so hard on yourself. If your parents aren't happy with it, so what?"

I raised an eyebrow. "Says the guy who jumps through hoops for his dad."

"Flaming hoops," he added. "And my situation's different."

"How?" I challenged him.

"My dad's way stricter than your folks," said Chase. "If I screw up, he probably has Understudy Chase waiting in the wings."

I leaned my head on his shoulder. "Yeah, well, *nobody* can replace you, so joke's on him," I said.

Chase rested his head on mine. "Thanks."

We sat in silence, listening to barking dogs and the whir of a lawnmower until I knew it was time to head home.

"I don't suppose the politician's son came up with something I could tell my parents?" I finally asked.

Chase stretched and said, "How about . . . the committee loved your audition and gave you the biggest supporting role you've *ever* had."

My lips slid into a grin. "Ooh. That's brilliant!"

"Thanks." He helped me to my feet. "Just don't tell my dad or he'll make me run for class president."

I fished in my backpack for a pen and notepad. "Say that whole thing again."

Chase recited as I wrote, and I practiced on him a few times while we walked toward my house.

"One last tip," he said when we reached my driveway. "If all else fails, use big positive words to describe your situation. Inspiring . . . a tour de force . . . stuff like that."

"Inspiring," I repeated. "A Tour de France."

"Tour de force," he corrected. "Tour de France is a bike race."

I wrinkled my forehead, trying to remember it all. "Why did my mom have to be an actress? Why couldn't she have been a lunch lady?"

Chase leaned in close. "Because guys don't like girls with tuna fish hair," he whispered.

I pushed him away with a smile. "Good-bye, Chase."

"Good luck," he said. "Let me know what happens."

I took a deep breath and climbed the porch steps, hoping that maybe my parents had developed amnesia or moved without telling me. But when I opened the front door, my mom emerged from the family room, grinning broadly.

"There's my superstar!" she said. "Come here, Sunny!" She held her arms open and I walked into them.

"Hi, Mommy." I hugged her, hoping she couldn't smell failure on me. "How was your day?"

"Very exciting!" she said, stepping back to take my hands. "You'll never guess who came to visit." She pulled me into the family room, and every muscle in my body tensed. There was only one other person in the world who cared as much about the play as my parents, and she was sitting beside my dad on the couch, sipping jasmine tea.

My grandmother.

Chocolate Monkey churned in my stomach. "Hey, Dad. Hey, Grandma," I said, summoning my most cheerful voice.

"Sunny!" Grandma pushed the teacup into my dad's

hands and hoisted herself off the couch to hug me. The second the greeting was over, she pulled away, her expression serious.

"What happened with the play?"

"Oh!" I laughed nervously. "Well . . . my friend on the selection committee said she loved my audition."

Grandma stared at me, unblinking. "And?"

I looked from her to my mom and dad, who were sitting on the edge of the couch, holding each other's hands.

Now was the time for some big positive words.

"Well, I was brilliant and mesmerizing and . . ." My palms were starting to sweat under Grandma's scrutinous gaze.

"Did you get a good part?" she pressed.

"I got a *great* part," I assured her. "It's the biggest part—"

"You got the biggest part?!" interrupted Grandma. She whooped with joy and turned to my parents. "She got the biggest part!"

Mom clasped her hands together and praised the sky, while Dad whistled through his fingers.

"Ohhh, shoot," I muttered.

Apparently, jumping to conclusions was a family thing.

THREE

EVEN WITH A SCRIPT FROM Chase I'd managed to botch things up. And I hadn't realized how much my family had been hoping for good news. Mom and Grandma were actually *tangoing* across the room.

"Wait," I said. "You've got it all wrong."

"She's right," said Grandma, pointing at Mom's feet. "You're off a step."

"No," I said. "I mean—"

Mom squished my face in her hands. "I'm so proud! My daughter . . . star of the school play!"

"But Mom," I forced the words through chubby cheeks. "It's not that big a—"

I was going to say "part," but *Dad* interrupted this time.

"Of course it's that big a deal!" he said, tousling my hair.

"We've waited forever!" added Grandma.

Dad shot her a warning look and Grandma shrugged. "It's true."

Mom waved her away and hugged me tight. "Tonight we'll do whatever you want to celebrate!"

At the moment all I *wanted* was to crawl into a hole and die. It was too late to tell them I didn't get the lead role. The truth would kill them, and then I'd be sent to prison, where nobody won an Oscar.

No, until I could think of something better, I'd have to pretend life was perfect and that my dream had come true.

Summoning a huge smile, I said, "Can we go to Guero's for dinner? All this excitement's made me hungry!"

Everyone laughed.

"Of course!" said Dad. "You've earned it."

I should have, for *that* performance. For good measure, I jumped up and down, clapping my hands and hating myself.

"Yay! Let me get ready!" I grabbed my bag and hurried upstairs. It was too dangerous to call Chase, so I texted him instead.

Help! Parents think I'm a star! I typed.

Guess those astronomy lessons were a waste, he responded.

"Chase!" I squeezed the phone in frustration. This was *no* time for jokes.

Someone knocked on the other side of my door and I froze.

"Everything okay?" called Mom.

"Yeah! I'm just changing!" I said, pulling on my jeans.

"We'll be in the car," said Mom. "Don't make us wait too long!"

"Be right out!" I told her. I started to type a response to Chase, but the phone vibrated with another message from him.

Okay, bad joke, he typed. *Set things straight. Gotta hang w/ my dad and defend theater. Good luck!*

With a frustrated sigh, I threw the phone in my purse. No way could I set things straight right now. Not with my family singing some Korean victory song in the driveway. I'd just have to act like I was a good actress.

Ironic.

The second I climbed in the car, my parents and grandmother started firing questions at me, wanting more details about the play.

"What's your rehearsal schedule?" asked Dad.

"When do rehearsals *start*?" asked Mom.

"Are you wearing another potato sack?" asked Grandma. "Because last time, I hugged you and got a rash."

Mom clapped a hand to her forehead and Dad turned his attention to the road.

"You know, I was just so excited, I forgot to ask." I laughed and shook my head. "I'll find out tomorrow."

Mom smiled and nodded, leaning back in her seat, but Grandma just stared at me.

"It took a month for the rash to go away," she said.

My phone vibrated in my bag and I jumped to answer it, hoping it was Chase. Unfortunately, the caller ID said Stefan. I ignored the insistent buzzing.

Grandma nudged me. "Answer the phone! It could be your drama teacher!"

"It's Stefan," I told her. "I'll call him back later."

Mom turned around. "He probably wants to know about the play results. You should give him the good news!"

"He *did* put a lot of effort into your audition," Dad chimed in.

"Fine," I said through clenched teeth, and answered the phone.

"Sunny!" chirped Stefan.

I took a deep breath, pasted on a wide grin, and said, "Hey, Stefan! What's up?"

"Do we have something to celebrate?" he asked.

My whole body stiffened, but I forced myself to keep smiling. "No, not at all!" I said. At the curious look from my family, I put my hand over the mouthpiece and told them, "He wants to know if he's interrupting."

"Ahhh," said my mother with a nod of understanding.

"Awww!" said Stefan with a tone of anguish. "They gave you a crappy little part again, didn't they?"

"They sure did!" I said with a laugh and a wink at my grandma.

"Well, this is crazy," said Stefan. "I'll talk to Ms. Elliott and figure out what happened. You did *not* deserve to be overlooked."

The smile on my face was genuine now.

"Thanks, Stefan," I said.

"I'll call you when I have info," he said and hung up.

I put my phone down and Grandma frowned.

"You done talking? He didn't want details?"

"Uh . . . no," I said, thinking fast. "He had to go. There was something burning on the stove."

"I didn't know Stefan could cook," said Mom.

"He can't. That's why it was burning. Look, there's Guero's!" I pointed out the window, grateful for a change of subject.

We pulled into the parking lot, and Dad walked around to my side.

"Celebrities first," he said, opening the door.

"Consider us your entourage," added Mom.

Two parents and an old lady with a potato sack allergy. That seemed like the kind of entourage I deserved.

"Thank you," I said, ducking my head modestly as I climbed out of the car.

Guero's was famous for their garlic bread, which I normally loved, but this time I couldn't bring myself to eat more than half a slice.

"You okay?" asked Mom, rubbing my shoulder. "I thought you liked the bread here."

"I'm fine," I said. "Chase and I shared a muffin after school. I guess I'm still kind of full."

She nodded and brushed my hair away from my face.

"We should ask Chase and his father over for dinner," said Dad. "I like talking politics with him."

"Sunny should marry the boy," said Grandma. "He would make a fine husband."

My parents exchanged looks, and I blushed.

"Grandma, I'm thirteen," I said. "And Chase and I aren't like that. We're just friends."

Grandma waggled a finger in my face. "Your grandfather and I were just friends. But then he gave me a pig."

I wrinkled my forehead. "That doesn't even make sense."

"Chase gave you a muffin," said Grandma.

"Because we're *friends*," I said again. "Not because he likes me. There're no farm animals in my future."

"Maybe not," Dad chimed in. "But what your grandmother says isn't that strange. Your mom even did a one-woman show about a princess who received cattle as marriage offers." He smiled and took Mom's hand. "What did you call it?"

She smiled back. "*The Cow Girl*."

Dad chuckled. "The people who went to see it were expecting a Western about cowgirls."

Everyone laughed, and I nibbled on garlic bread, picturing my mom in a one-woman show. She would have been the top-billed and *only* star, every actress's ultimate dream. I could only hope someday—

Wait! Why not now?

I gasped in excitement and inhaled a bite of bread.

When I started coughing, everyone glanced over in alarm, and Grandma whacked me on the back. Before she could break my spine, I gave a thumbs-up and took a long drink of soda.

"Are you okay?" asked Mom.

I nodded.

I was *more* than okay. I was brilliant!

The moment I got home, I called Stefan. My plan was way too exciting to wait until after he'd talked to Ms. Elliott.

If CAA wasn't going to choose me to star in any of their shows, I'd just have to star in my own. That way, I'd be telling my family the truth *and* I'd get the part I always wanted. Plus, I was pretty sure nobody in CAA history had ever attempted a one-girl show. I'd be a legend!

"Hello?" said Stefan over a background madness of barking and squawking.

His parents owned a cute pet shop called Feathers 'N' Fangs, and sometimes he covered the register.

"Stefan?" I asked. "Are you at work?"

"Yeah, but with all the whining and screeching, it could just as easily be *Idol* auditions."

I laughed. "Why don't you tell the animals to be quiet?"

"I can't. When I raise my voice, the rabbits freak out

and go bald," he said. "What's up? I haven't called Ms. Elliott yet."

"That's fine," I said, settling on the floor by my bed. "I've got an even better plan that'll make me famous."

"Uh-oh," said Stefan. "You're not going to jump off the roof with a cape again, are you?"

"Of course not." I lifted the corner of my comforter and ducked under it, pushing aside a stack of DVDs to look for scripts. One of the perks of having parents in the film business was access to loads of movie junk. "What would you say if I told you I was doing a one-girl show?"

Stefan gasped. "I'd say you're *brilliant*!" He paused. "Oops. A rabbit just lost some fur."

I pulled a stack of scripts into my lap and flipped through them. "I could use help, though," I said. "I'm not sure what piece to do. You think I should ask Bree too?"

She knew every play from *Annie* to *Ziegfeld Girl*.

"I think first you should clear your idea with Ms. Elliott," said Stefan.

I paused. "Oh . . . right." A feeling of dread crept up my spine. "You don't think she'll say no, do you?"

"Maybe," he said. "You're competing for stage time with the *Mary Pops In* cast."

"Right," I said again, biting my lip. I hadn't seen much

of the script, but from what I'd heard, there were at least three dance numbers, including the chimney sweep waltz and a hip-hop dance to "Tuppence a Bag, Y'all."

"Okay, I'll talk to her tomorrow morning," I said.

"Great! Keep me posted?" Stefan asked.

"Of course!" I said, with more enthusiasm than I actually felt. Asking Ms. Elliott's permission had been the last thing on my mind. If she wouldn't let me do my show, I was sunk.

With a heavy sigh, I hefted my scripts onto the bed and joined them, tucking my stuffed dog Rufus under one arm. I was too old for toys, but he was the closest thing to a pet I'd ever had . . . other than one poor, trampled hamster.

My parents bought Rufus when I was five, swearing that he came to life at bedtime. I probably would have believed it forever if I hadn't accidentally popped out one of Rufus's eyes.

To keep me from needing extensive therapy, my parents confessed that he wasn't real and that Dad was allergic to dogs. They'd lied about Rufus to spare my feelings.

At the time I'd been furious, but now that I was in their shoes I kind of understood why they did it.

Sometimes you just couldn't disappoint family.

FOUR

AT LEAST A DOZEN BUTTERFLIES were swooping through my stomach the next morning, making it impossible to eat breakfast. While I pushed soggy wheat squares around in my bowl, I wrote and crossed out a dozen ways to convince Ms. Elliott to give me my own show.

~~*Ms. Elliott, I really really really want*~~

~~*Ms. Elliott, my life will be ruined if*~~

Want to see your precious poodle again? Then—

"What's that?" asked Grandma, shuffling over to the table.

I flipped my notebook closed. "Math. I love it." Nobody would believe that. "I mean, a love note." She'd think it was for Chase. "I mean, a love note to my math teacher."

Awkward. Very awkward.

Grandma raised an eyebrow. "No, what's *that*?" She pointed at my cereal. "You're eating wallpaper paste?"

"Oh!" I laughed and glanced at the bowl. "I guess it does look pretty gross. I wasn't hungry."

Grandma studied me. "You didn't eat much dinner either."

"I'm just really nervous about this play," I said. "It's my first big part!"

I gave her a wide smile, hoping that would hold her off. After a moment she nodded and patted my shoulder.

"Don't forget to get details," she said. "And leave your math teacher alone."

I cringed but nodded and shoved the notebook in my bag. "Would you tell Mom and Dad I left early? I need to talk to Ms. Elliott before school starts."

Grandma agreed, and I was out the door. The sooner my lie was behind me, the better.

Even though I reached campus early, CAA was already buzzing with activity. Our ballet troupe practiced at sunrise so the boys couldn't sneak into the studio and whistle at them. Other students showed up to finish art projects or practice solos in private.

With every step closer to Ms. Elliott's office, my heart beat faster, and far too soon, I was rounding the corner to the faculty hall. Ms. Elliott's door was open and the light was on. It was now or never.

I stepped through her doorway . . . and froze.

Ms. Elliott had her winged back to me. Her *winged* back. And she was fluttering her arms as she flitted over to one of the plants in her office with a watering can.

I cleared my throat, and she stumbled, almost knocking over a fern. With a quick glance at me, she smiled sheepishly.

"Excuse me," she said, standing upright. "I was embracing my inner fairy queen. Another role I'm trying for in the city play."

"Wouldn't fairy queens have fairy gardeners to take care of their plants?" I asked.

She winked at me and put down her watering can. "You are as bright as your name, Sunny. To what do I owe this lovely visit?"

I sat in a chair across from her desk. "Things didn't go well at the *Mary Pops In* tryouts," I said.

"On the contrary, I hear from this year's committee that you've shown marked improvement," said Ms. Elliott with a smile. "Unfortunately, I also hear the competition was fierce."

I fought back an argument and said, "That's not really why I'm here. Ms. Elliott, I want to do a one-girl show apart from the semester play. An . . . an independent student project," I added, remembering Chase's words.

"A one-girl show?" Ms. Elliott settled into her desk chair and sipped from her coffee mug. "Tell me more."

My heart gave a happy leap, and I pulled some scripts out of my bag.

"I've got all these ideas," I said. "If I'm not the right person for an existing role, I'd at least like a chance to try one *I've* selected."

Ms. Elliott reached for the scripts and studied them. Then she studied me. "If this is an independent project, you'll have to do this without my help. And it needs to be completed by the time *Mary Pops In* debuts."

"So . . . you're . . ." I held my breath. Was she saying yes?

Ms. Elliott picked up her mug and watched me. "When the theater group isn't using the stage, you may use it," she said. "I can give you a small budget for additional items: makeup, music, costuming, but you'll have to provide some things on your own."

I stared at her, waiting for a bigger catch.

Ms. Elliott misunderstood my hesitation. "Sunny, if you can't accept—"

I jumped to my feet. “No, I can! I totally can!”

“Well . . . good.” She leaned away, startled by my enthusiasm.

I cleared my throat and sat back down. “I can really have my own show?”

Ms. Elliott finally smiled. “I admire your tenacity, Sunny. And you’re right. You do deserve a chance.”

I could’ve jumped up and hugged her, but Ms. Elliott had a tight grip on her coffee mug and looked ready to splash me.

“Thank you so much,” I said, standing with slow dignity. “I promise it’ll be a *great* show.”

If I’d been wearing Ms. Elliott’s wings, I could have soared through the halls, lightheaded with giddiness . . . and hunger. Now that my stomach wasn’t twisted with worry, I was starting to wish I’d eaten that bowl of wallpaper paste.

There were still twenty minutes before first class, so I headed for the cafeteria to celebrate my victory with a mound of French toast. Just as I joined the serving line, Bree stepped up behind me.

“Hey, Sunny,” she said.

“Bree!” I exclaimed. “Great news!”

“Everyone in *Mary Pops In* got laryngitis?” she asked with a little smile.

"Better," I said, grabbing her arms. "I'm gonna put on a show!"

"A show?" Bree tilted her head, confused. "Here in line?"

"No!" I laughed. "Instead of the school play. I asked Ms. Elliott if I could do my own show, and she said yes!"

Bree's eyes widened. "That's *awesome*."

"I was hoping you'd say that," I said, holding out my scripts. "Because I wanted to ask—"

"Yes!" She gasped, the loudest sound I'd ever heard her make. "Oh, Sunny, I'd love to be in your show!"

Whoops.

I took a step back. "Uh . . . Bree, no. I'm really sorry, but this is going to be just me . . . a one-girl show."

Bree let her tray clatter onto the serving rail. "Figures. My second rejection of the week," she said. "At least I'm great at *that*."

I squeezed her arm. "I'm really sorry," I said again. "Do you want me to ask Ms. Elliott if you could do your own show, too?"

Bree shook her head. "She'd never let me. Everyone says I'm so quiet, I make snow sound loud."

I grimaced. "Awww. You're not *that* . . ." I trailed off and reached for a basket of French toast sticks.

Instead of grabbing food, Bree clasped her hands in front of her and looked at me with puppy dog eyes. "Please, Sunny. Let me be in your show."

I sighed. "Bree—"

"What show?" Suresh, Bree's boyfriend, leaned over her shoulder.

"Sunny's putting on a production," said Bree. "Ms. Elliott approved it and everything."

"That's great!" said Suresh.

And then he said the six words I was dreading to hear.

"I want to be in it."

"It's a *one-girl* show," I said, paying for my food.

He shrugged. "I can dress like a girl."

I gave him a look and picked up my tray. "You're missing the point. It's a *one*-person show."

I walked away from the line, and Bree and Suresh followed.

"Come on, Sunny. Please?" he said. "I'm trying to bring in Bollywood."

I picked up my fork. "That's great, but—"

"Everyone thinks I'm here on a snake-charming scholarship," he added. "And I can't tell you how many kids want me to teach them yoga. And—"

"I get it," I said. "You're a walking stereotype."

He nodded enthusiastically. "But if I had a legitimate acting role, I could make them understand."

"Me too!" piped up Bree. "Then maybe kids would stop leaving cue cards that say *LOUDER* in my locker."

I held up a hand to silence them. "Listen, I'll go to Ms. Elliott and see if you guys can have your *own* show. She can't possibly say no."

And I was right.

When I visited Ms. Elliott at noon, she didn't say no. She said, "Absolutely not."

The confident smile I'd worn into her office faded. "What? How come?" I asked.

Ms. Elliott adjusted her glasses. "Sunny, I was fine letting you have your own show because I thought that would be the end of it. But if I let Bree and Suresh have their own show too, then I have to let the next students. Soon there won't be enough stage time for all of you."

"Then say no to anyone *after* Bree and Suresh," I said with a hopeful smile.

She shook her head. "I'm sorry, you'll just have to let them into your production."

"Let them . . ." My mouth fell open. "But this is *my* chance for fame and glory!"

"I'm afraid that's all I can offer," she said. "You either

tell them no or share the stage. Now"—she held up two wigs—"which of these says fairy queen?"

"The purple," I mumbled, picking up my backpack.

There was no floating through the halls with giddiness this time. Instead, there were shackles of guilt around each ankle, one for not getting Bree and Suresh their show and another for not wanting them to be in mine.

To make my conscience feel better, I went in search of the one person who could tell me the right thing to do.

"Chase?" I called, rounding the corner of his locker bay. "You won't believe—"

I stopped short. Not because he wasn't there, but because he was there with Ilana. And she was wearing his jacket. And giggling.

I don't know why it bothered me. I had no desire to wear Chase's jacket, he wasn't my boyfriend, and she wasn't my best friend. But I had a sudden urge to pull him away from her.

Chase smiled at me. "Hey, Sunny D! What's up?"

"Can we talk?" I asked him, giving Ilana a small smile.

In response she propped her cosmetics case in one arm and held open the lid. "Makeover while you chat?" She gestured at the contents. "You could look *killer*."

I shook my head. "I don't want to look like a killer. Just give me a second with Chase, please?"

Chase raised his eyebrows, and Ilana snapped her case shut.

"Fine," she said, stepping between Chase and me. She gazed up at him and smiled sweetly. "See you this afternoon?" she asked.

"Of course!" he said. "And thanks for the history notes." He saluted her with a hot pink binder.

"Thank *you* for the ten bucks," she said, patting her pocket as she sauntered away.

"What's happening this afternoon?" I asked, watching her leave.

"Ilana's coming to my baseball practice," he said with a pleased smile. "You want to come?"

"Uh . . ." I chewed my lip. "If I say yes, do I have to actually show up?"

Chase rolled his eyes. "Never mind. What's going on?"

"I have a moral dilemma I need help with," I said.

His expression turned serious. "Yes, you *should* leave tap dancing off your list of theater skills."

I scowled at him. "My dancing is fine. I just didn't know the edge of the stage was so close."

"Then I'd leave 'observant' off your list of theater skills," said Chase.

I gasped in mock dismay and raised a fist. Chase laughed and threw his arms up protectively, spilling papers out of Ilana's binder. We both bent to grab them.

"All right, I'll be serious," he said, sliding the papers back into the folder pocket. "What's your moral dilemma?"

"Huh?" My attention was now on one of the papers in my hand.

Audition Assessment . . . MPI, it said. Below that was a list of comments in different handwritings and different colored pens.

This was an audition evaluation for *Mary Pops In*!

I shifted it aside and saw another one underneath.

"What's that?" asked Chase.

I jumped up and held the papers against my chest. "Some homework of mine that Ilana borrowed. Small world, huh?" I laughed loudly and grabbed the binder from Chase. "What else is in there?"

"Just lab notes and poetry about her mom."

"Oh. Lame." I thrust the binder back at him.

"I'd leave 'compassionate' off the résumé too," said Chase.

"Uh-huh," I said absentmindedly. "Well, I've gotta go.

Later!" With the pages still pressed to my chest, I walked away at a hurried pace.

"Hey!" Chase called. "I thought you had a question!"

"I do!" I shouted over my shoulder.

The question was . . . what did the audition assessments say?

FIVE

I COULD BARELY FOCUS IN MATH, with the stack of assessments taunting me from my notebook. The moment the teacher let us do busy work, I pounced on the first review . . . Bree's.

It started out okay, even though her name was spelled B-r-i-e, like the cheese. She'd been rated highly on emotion and style, but under stage presence and vocals, there were a series of back-and-forth comments.

Is she talking? I can't hear her.

My eyebrows rose. That was Ilana's handwriting.

She's quiet but good! Someone else wrote in pink pen.

Maybe if she gestured more with her hands? Another person suggested in blue.

Forget it, wrote Ilana. *This isn't* Mime-y Poppins. *She won't work as a lead.*

I frowned at the assessment. Bree *was* quiet, but if she had a microphone, she'd be fine. Ilana needed to give her some credit.

I shifted that assessment to the back and looked at the next one for a boy named Max. Again, the first comment was from Ilana.

Does he have to shout everything? Although . . . between him and Brie, we'd have a normal-sounding person.

"Awww!" I said out loud. At a look from my algebra teacher, I added, "Curse you, stupid equation!"

The teacher frowned but turned away, and I went back to reading Max's assessment.

But he's cute! commented the judge with the pink pen.

Plus, he's funny, added the blue.

Yeah, and he could shatter glass with his voice, wrote Ilana. *Make him a village kid.*

I glanced at Ilana, who was giving her makeover pitch to a girl in orange lipstick. Considering what she'd said about not having control, she seemed to be calling a lot of the shots on casting.

I read the other assessments, and the pattern was the same. Thoughtful comments from her co-judges and thinly veiled insults from Ilana. Every rejection was for some reason that *might* make a little sense if it wasn't so incredibly shallow.

At the bottom of the pile, I found mine.

Cute! She'd be good as the housekeeper, wrote Ilana.

The *housekeeper*? I snapped my head up to glare in her direction.

Ilana hadn't suggested me for Mary Poppins at all!

I returned to the page to see what the others had to say.

We already have that role filled, wrote Pink Pen. *How about Jane Banks?*

Or even Mary Poppins? suggested Blue Pen. *Sunny's a pretty good singer.*

I felt a momentary surge of satisfaction that at least *someone* had considered me for a lead role.

But then I saw Ilana's next comment.

Jane Banks can't be Asian with white parents. It's not normal. And an Asian Mary Poppins would just be weird.

"What?!" I shouted. "Are you kidding me?"

The math teacher scowled and pointed at the door.

"That's enough for one class. Principal's office," she said.

I knew there was no chance for redemption, so I grabbed my stuff and headed toward the door. On my way out I slapped the audition assessments on Ilana's desk.

"See you at Chase's practice" was all I said.

My walk home after school was a blur, each step turbo-fueled by anger. I'd never felt more betrayed than I did by Ilana at that moment. A few times came close, like when my parents told me swearing killed the dinosaurs, but at least *they* hadn't done it for shallow, evil reasons.

Plus, the principal still remembered me from his wig-tastrophe, so I'd gotten Saturday detention for the second time that year, which would *not* please my parents. Asian Bad Girl was a role they wouldn't have me play unless it came with the chance for an Emmy.

I wanted to get home to an empty house, but to my ultra irritation, I smelled kimchi the second I opened the front door. While I normally love Korean food, spicy pickled cabbage is *not* a soothing scent, and it could only mean Grandma was still lingering.

Sure enough, only a few seconds passed before she stepped into the living room and beckoned me to the kitchen. I followed, dropping my bag on the counter.

A huge glass jar sat on the dining table, packed with red chili juice and white cabbage. Two steaming bowls of rice waited beside them.

"Your parents are out meeting a friend," she said. "They may have a surprise for you soon."

"Oh." I didn't have the heart to act excited. "That's nice."

Grandma handed me a bowl of rice and a fork to spear the kimchi. "You don't like surprises?" she asked.

"Not unless it's Ilana Rourke's head on a stick." I stabbed a piece of cabbage and ate it straight from the jar.

Grandma watched me. "I don't understand."

I shook my head and mumbled around a mouthful of rice. "It's not important."

I swallowed a second bite of rice to tone down the spiciness of the kimchi. The sides of my nose had started to sweat. Grandma nodded and sat down, scooping some cabbage from the jar for herself.

"How was school?" she asked. The look on her face was genuinely concerned, so I forced a smile.

"Fine," I said. "The usual eighth-grade hijinks."

"Ah. And what did you learn about the *play*?" asked Grandma.

I stopped chewing. In all the madness over Ilana and my one-girl show, I'd forgotten to create an alibi.

But it *was* my show. Why couldn't I just make up a schedule?

"We meet after school, and rehearsals start Thursday," I told Grandma.

My lips tingled, and my tongue felt like it was on fire. I tried to cool it with a sip of water, holding it in my mouth.

Grandma leaned forward. "Spicy, isn't it?"

I nodded and gulped half the glass of water.

"That's what happens with Truth Kimchi," said Grandma. She dabbed at her mouth with a napkin while I wiped at my forehead with a sleeve.

"Truth Kimchi?" I repeated.

Grandma narrowed her eyes wisely. "Ancient recipe. Every time you lie, it gets hotter," she said.

My stomach gurgled uncomfortably. "Well, it's not that hot," I said. To prove it, I slid another piece of fiery cabbage in my mouth. Grandma took two pieces and ate them solemnly, watching me.

"Your eye always twitches like that?" she asked. "And your nose leaks?"

I sniffed deeply and opened my eyes wider, blinking rapidly. "Just allergies," I said. Tiny fireballs threatened to shoot from my mouth.

Grandma smiled widely and shoveled a stack of kimchi into my bowl. "Eat this. It clears sinuses."

I looked down at my bowl and laughed nervously. If Grandma kept up the questions, the Truth Kimchi was going to burn a hole through my stomach.

Of course, there was always the possibility she was tricking me.

"I don't believe this is really Truth Kimchi," I said, though the words were garbled with my tongue pressed to a napkin.

"No?" asked Grandma. She reached under the table and produced a bottle of thick golden liquid. "Then this isn't really antidote."

She poured a little into my empty water glass, and I sniffed at it before taking a sip. After a few seconds, the burning sensation in my mouth subsided. I breathed contentedly and let her pour the rest.

"Now that we know you are lying, why don't we start over?" asked Grandma.

I slunk down in my seat, red-faced from both the kimchi and embarrassment. My brain worked overtime, trying to figure out how I could talk about Ilana and my one-girl show without admitting I wasn't the star of *Mary Pops In*.

Grandma leaned closer. "I know you're not the star."

My glass slipped and hit the table. That was one secret out of the way.

"Yes, fine," I said, righting my glass. "I'm just an extra, but it's the biggest part I've ever gotten. And when you guys thought it was the biggest part *period*, I couldn't correct you." I focused on my glass and swirled the golden residue around the bottom. "I didn't want you to be disappointed again."

"Sunny." Grandma covered my hand with hers. "We are disappointed only if you give up," she said with a smile. "Because you try, we are always proud."

My eyes watered again, but it wasn't because of the kimchi. "Thanks, Grandma," I said.

She squeezed my hand and let it go. "So you didn't get the part," she said. "Did the committee give a reason?"

I made a face. "That's why I'm mad at Ilana. She's *supposed* to be my friend, but she wouldn't cast me because 'an Asian Mary Poppins would just be weird.'" I snorted and rolled my eyes. "Crazy, right?"

Grandma rubbed her chin with a finger and shook her head. "Not crazy. Disappointing." She got up and carried the kimchi jar into the kitchen.

I turned to watch. "What's that mean?"

Grandma's eyes narrowed shrewdly. "Ilana is a good actress but she judges people. I hear her talking after last year's show."

My forehead wrinkled. "You did? Where was I?"

"Hugging people and giving them rashes," said Grandma with a frown.

I rolled my eyes. "*Sorry*. What did Ilana say?"

Grandma hesitated then sighed. "She says the heavy girl with the pretty voice takes up too much stage. And the boy with the stutter makes the show last an hour longer."

I winced even though the verbal jabs hadn't been directed at me. I knew the kids she was talking about, Anne Marie and Cole. They were really sweet and definitely didn't deserve that.

"Maybe we should move," I told Grandma. "To a city where nobody judges."

Grandma laughed and poured the kimchi down the drain. "That is make-believe. No matter where you go, there is judgment. Too rich, too poor, too young, too old . . . even in your magazines." She nodded at one that had slid out of my backpack. "You think the cover shows heavy people?"

I glanced at the copy of *Style Now*. A gorgeous, slender girl smiled up from the front cover.

"That doesn't make it right," I said.

"I agree," said Grandma, filling the jar with water and soap. "But it is the way things are."

I tossed the magazine on the counter. After all the hard work I'd put into my audition, that answer was *not* the right one.

"If nobody else wants to change things, then *I* will," I said. "Tell Mom and Dad I'll be back in a few hours."

Grandma looked up in surprise. "Where are you going?"

"To confront Ilana." I burped and made a face. "After I brush my teeth."

She nodded, and I started for the staircase, then paused. "I guess the Truth Kimchi really works. You should have kept some."

Grandma smiled. "There is no Truth Kimchi. Just extra hot peppers."

I smiled back. "You tricked me!"

"I *outsmarted* you," she said, holding up a finger. "Big difference."

"How?"

"If I trick my granddaughter, I'm mean," said Grandma with a wink. "If I outsmart her, I'm wise."

I laughed and ran upstairs to prep for my showdown with Ilana. If things were gonna get *West Side Story*, I'd need my toughest pair of boots and my skull T-shirt. Granted, it was a skull decorated with pink rhinestones, but the message was clear.

Nobody messed with Villager Number Two.

SIX

ONE BUS RIDE LATER I was climbing into the bleachers at the ball field. Ilana was sitting with a few girls, cosmetic case on her lap, and as soon as she spotted me, she nudged the girls on either side of her. They stopped talking and eyed me warily.

I nodded at Ilana's friends. "Would you mind leaving for a second?"

Ilana whirled around to give them a *don't you dare* look, and they glanced at one another nervously.

I crossed my hands over my chest. "Or I can show you a new face kick I learned in Tae Kwon Do."

"Bye!" one of the girls blurted, and fled the stands. The others scrambled after her.

I didn't really know Tae Kwon Do, but people seemed to think "Asian" equaled martial arts expert. I could have told the girls I was a ninja, and they would have believed it.

Ilana watched her friends bail, then laughed nervously. "You know, I promised one of them a makeover, so I should . . ."

She got up to leave, and I stepped in her path.

"Sit."

"Right." She dropped back onto the bench.

"I saw those mean things you wrote about people in the audition assessments," I said.

Ilana had the nerve to look offended. "Not mean. Truthful. And why do you care? I didn't say anything bad about *you*."

My eyes widened. "You said I couldn't be Mary Poppins because I'm Asian!" I exclaimed.

People sitting nearby glanced over. Ilana blushed and tried to defend herself.

"An Asian Mary Poppins isn't believable," she said.

I clapped a hand to my forehead. "Mary Poppins uses an *umbrella* to fly around London and hops into chalk drawings. How is *that* any more believable?"

Ilana turned up her nose. "It's understood that she's a little different."

"Then why not make her Asian?" I asked.

"Because that's a *lot* different!" said Ilana. "People want what's familiar."

I raised an eyebrow. "We're talking about *Mary Pops In*. A musical where 'A Spoonful of Sugar' is now 'A Canful of Cola.'"

Ilana waved my argument away. "That's nothing."

"Ilana, come *on*!" I cried. This time, it was loud enough for some of the players to hear, including Chase.

He frowned, and I gave a nervous wave before sitting beside Ilana.

"Fine, so you didn't pick me," I said in a softer voice, "but there were a bunch of people way better than Sara for that role."

Ilana shook her head. "Nope. They all had huge flaws that would *destroy* the show. And it has to be a perfect performance."

I tried to remember all the things I'd read on the evaluations. "How is . . . a girl who gestures too much going to destroy the show?"

"She could knock over scenery," Ilana answered.

"And a girl who spits when she talks?" I asked.

"She could drown the audience," said Ilana.

I groaned. "That's ridiculous. And it's not fair."

"Life's not fair," Ilana said flatly. "If it was, I wouldn't—" She cut herself off. "Just let it go, Sunny, and wait for high school."

"Wait for high school?!" I jumped to my feet, and Ilana flinched.

If Chase hadn't appeared just then, I'm not sure what would have happened. Ilana probably would've been sporting a bald spot.

"Hey, guys, thanks for coming!" Chase said, stepping between us. To me, he turned and said in a hoarse whisper, "What's with the yelling?"

"I'm not yelling," I said. "I'm calling Ilana out for being a jerk." I leaned past him so she could hear me. "With all the money you earn on makeovers, you'd think you could buy a better personality!"

"Sunny!" Chase said with a shocked look.

I held up a hand to stop him. "Do you know what she did?"

"I don't care," he said, pushing my hand aside. "That was really harsh. You probably hurt her feelings."

We both turned toward Ilana, who was staring at the ground with a forlorn expression.

"See?" he said.

"She's faking. All good actresses can do that," I said, but I wasn't sure.

"I think you should leave," said Chase with a frown. "Especially since you don't have any real interest in watching *me* play."

Now he looked almost as hurt as Ilana. How did *I* suddenly become the bad guy?

I grabbed his hand. "Chase, I'm sorry, but you should have seen her tearing people apart at auditions! And she wouldn't pick *me* for Mary Poppins because I'm Asian."

Chase studied me, and for a second I thought I'd won him back to my side. But then he shook his head.

"Ilana wasn't the only person on the selection committee. There could've been other reasons they didn't pick you."

"But—"

"Stop it, Sunny!" Chase scowled. "You didn't get the part. Let it go!"

His words stunned me into silence, and I pressed my lips together to fight back tears. Chase had *always* tried to see my side, but now that he and Ilana were getting close, there was no reason to.

"For your information," I finally said, glaring at him, "I

don't want that stupid part anymore. Not if it means spending time around you."

Chase opened his mouth to speak, but I cut him off.

"Besides," I said, "Ms. Elliott's letting me star in my *own* show, so I won't have the time."

His eyebrows lifted. "Really?" he asked.

Ilana stepped forward. "Excuse me?"

"That's right." I nodded, feeling a new surge of conviction.

Forget the one-girl show. I had something bigger to prove.

"And unlike the cast *you* selected, mine will be chosen for the right reasons." I scowled at them and stormed out of the bleachers.

Now I had a problem.

How was I going to cast an entire production by myself? My theater experience was limited to classes and what I'd learned inside a potato sack. I didn't really feel qualified to hold auditions. What I really needed was a seasoned professional. Someone like . . .

"Stefan?" I said when he answered his phone. "Do you have a second?"

"I'm watching the shop, so I have all night," he said over the din of animal madness. "Come on by."

• • •

I called Mom to get me at the pet shop in an hour and walked the couple blocks to Feathers 'N' Fangs. When I opened the door, overhead bells jangled and a barrage of sound came from the side kennels. But nobody showed up to greet me.

"Hello!" I called.

A cage beside me rattled, and I jumped.

"Hell-o!" said a screechy voice.

I glanced over to see a parrot shifting from foot to foot.

"Hello!" I said again with a smile.

"Hell-o!" the parrot repeated.

Glancing around, I leaned closer.

"Sunny is a superstar," I said.

The parrot gave a throaty chuckle.

I couldn't even get respect from a bird.

"Don't mind Petie," said Stefan, emerging from the pet-food aisle. "He only knows 'hello.' Everything else gets a laugh." He reached into his apron pocket and pulled out a bird treat. "Right, Petie?"

As if in answer Petie let out another chuckle and poked his beak through the bars for the treat.

Stefan winked at me, and I smiled.

If I could've had anyone for a big brother, it would've

been him. He was tall and handsome, with a killer smile and hair gelled into short spikes. He looked born for show biz. Even in a ratty green apron.

"What do you say, protégé?" He held open his arms for a hug. "I'm sorry you didn't get Mary Poppins."

"I'm over it," I said, hugging him back.

"Please. You're in theater." Stefan grinned. "'Never forgive' is our sacred motto."

I made a face and stepped away. "Okay, fine. But I do have good news."

His grin deepened. "You got your one-girl show."

I rubbed my nails on my shirt. "Maybe."

Stefan laughed and applauded me. "Bravo. And did you decide on a piece?"

I lowered my hand. "Here's the thing."

He stopped laughing. "Uh-oh."

"It's not a one-girl show anymore," I said. "I'm letting other kids try out."

The bells over the shop door jangled, and Stefan waved at whoever walked in before returning his attention to me.

"That's sweet, but you realize more people on stage means less focus on you," he said.

"I know," I said. "But those kids never stood a chance at regular auditions."

While Stefan restocked dog biscuits, I told him about Ilana and the evaluations. His reaction was similar to Grandma's, but from the way he shoved boxes onto the shelf, I could tell he was more upset.

"I've seen that attitude at the high school level," he said, "but I hoped you were immune to it at your age."

"Nope," I said, repositioning the boxes. When I'd straightened them all, I stood there, staring at the shelf. "Maybe it's more than just discrimination, though." I turned to Stefan. "What if I didn't deserve anything better than an extra?"

Stefan gave me a withering look. "Don't be stupid. I was there, and you did great." He put a hand on my shoulder. "It's *possible* that Mary Poppins wasn't the best role for you, but you still deserved to be one of the leads."

"You think so?" I said, tracing the edges of a box with my fingers.

"Yes." Stefan arranged cans of dog food on the shelf. "But it doesn't matter what *I* think about you. It matters what *you* think about yourself."

I studied him for a minute. "That's serious wisdom from a guy shelving cans upside down."

"What?" Stefan stepped back to survey his work. "Yep. I've stocked an entire row with doof god."

We both laughed, and I helped him set the cans right side up.

"You just wait, Sunny," he said. "Once you step into that spotlight, you'll see you're a natural fit."

I stood on tiptoe to kiss his cheek. "You always have the right answers, Best Mentor Ever. Which is why I know you're going to say 'Yes' to my next question."

Stefan turned to face me. "Do I have a choice?"

"Of course," I said. "You can choose to say yes, or you can choose to *not* say no."

He smirked. "What's the favor?"

"I could use someone to help me judge the auditions," I said. "Someone with more theater experience who can give unbiased opinions."

Stefan grimaced. "Sorry, but I've got my own audition to worry about tomorrow afternoon. High school does theater too, you know."

I bit my lip. "What about tomorrow at lunch?" I asked. "You're allowed to leave campus, right?"

Stefan raised an eyebrow. "Yeah, but that doesn't give you a lot of time to announce auditions."

I waved his argument away. "Trust me. Everyone will find out."

"Then, sure," he said with a shrug. "I can help."

"Thank you!" I hugged him as the bells over the shop door jangled again.

"Give me a sec," said Stefan, disappearing toward the front. He came back a moment later, looking bewildered, with my mom in tow.

"Hey, Mom," I said. I gave Stefan a worried glance. "Is everything okay?"

Mom rushed forward and took my hands. "I just told him your big news!" she gushed.

I tilted my head to one side. "About me starring in a play? He already knows."

She laughed and hugged me. "No, not about the play! I mean . . . yes, about the play. But not about the *play*."

I eyed her suspiciously. "Did you have a stroke or something?"

Mom laughed again and shook her head. "I know I'm not making any sense, but I'm just so excited for you." She breathed deeply. "I was having lunch with friends today and bragging about your success."

"Really?" I asked.

Behind my mom, Stefan gave me a look and used his fingers to pull his face into a big smile.

"I mean . . . awww, thanks, Mom!" I said, beaming at her.

Luckily, she was too distracted to notice.

"Well, my friends were saying how nice it was that you're following in my footsteps," she continued. "And I realized, if that's true, why not start you off early?"

I shot Stefan a quick look, and he winked.

"What do you mean?" I asked Mom.

She took my hands. "I mean that I made some calls, and if everything goes well with your show, you might . . . just . . . get . . . an agent."

I didn't need cues from Stefan on how to react to *that*. The poor animals in the pet shop . . . so unprepared for my screams of joy.

"*What?!*" I shrieked, squeezing the life out of my mom's hands. "Are you serious?"

She nodded. "My friend Evelyn will be sitting in on your opening night. If that's okay with you."

"Of course it's okay!" I threw my arms around Mom, and she laughed.

"So you'll practice hard and make me proud," said Mom. "I want you to be the best Mary Poppins there is."

My muscles tensed. "Well—"

"She's going to be the star of the show!" interrupted Stefan. "Just you wait and see."

Mom pulled back and beamed from Stefan to me. "You ready to go?"

"Sure, in just a sec," I said. "Stefan was going to show me a kitten." I smiled and pushed him down the aisle.

"Hurry!" Mom called after us. "We have to get home for dinner."

I flashed her an okay sign, then used the same fingers to pinch Stefan's arm as soon as we were out of sight.

"Ow! What's with the talons?" he asked, rubbing the sore spot.

"The agent is coming to see me as the lead in *Mary Pops In*!" I hissed.

Stefan placed a hand on mine. "You're missing the point. The agent is coming to see you as the lead, *period.* Who cares if it's for a different production?"

"Well . . ."

"Once everything's worked out, you can tell your folks about the show," he continued. "But for now, just keep it under wraps."

I leaned against the wall and sighed. "Fine. But do me a favor. Call Bree and tell her about the auditions tomorrow.

I won't be able to get away to do it, and Bree will make sure everyone knows." I took a pen out of my purse and wrote down Bree's number.

"Sunny?" Mom appeared at the end of the aisle. "Let's get going."

"You heard the woman," I told Stefan, handing over the paper. "Let's get going."

SEVEN

THE NEXT MORNING BREE AND I were nearly trampled by a group of kids running through the hall. We leapt to either side of the crowd, and I clutched my backpack to my chest like a shield.

"What's going on?" I asked a girl named Janice (the one Ilana said spit when she talked).

Janice saw me and laughed. "Like you don't know."

Of course I did, but I wanted to be sure. It was hard to believe all these people were spreading the word about my show when I'd only just opened auditions the night before.

When the crowd passed, Bree and I rejoined and watched the last kid disappear around the corner.

"Did you see how many there were?" I asked. "Do you think they'll all try out?"

"Probably," said Bree with a shrug. "What have they got to lose?"

I took a deep breath. "Let's get some breakfast while I can still eat."

Stefan would show up at lunch to help out, but I wished Chase could come too. I knew it wouldn't happen, though, since we were fighting. Plus, he was too busy falling in *looove* with Ilana, my new archenemy.

When Bree and I entered the cafeteria, the happy couple was already there, sitting side by side at a table. They were sharing a book and laughing, but at the sound of our footsteps, Chase stopped and glanced up.

The last thing I needed was for him to think I felt guilty or wanted to apologize. I lowered my gaze and swept past, playing it cool all the way up until I crashed into someone at the milk fridge.

"Sorry!" I lifted my head to see Derek Green, one of the school's biggest deviants, frowning at me. Chocolate milk dribbled down his shirt. "Oh! Really, really sorry!"

I wiped at the mess with my sleeve, spreading the stain even further.

"Let me get a napkin or a . . . um . . . dry cleaner," I said, nodding to Bree. She ran off . . . for help, I hoped.

"Don't bother," said Derek, drinking what was left of his milk.

I glanced up nervously. "B-because when you pummel me, the shirt'll get bloody anyway?"

Derek sputtered and choked. "You say that *while* my mouth is full?" he asked.

"Sorry," I said, wringing my hands. "I normally don't talk to your type beyond 'Please, please, don't kill me.'"

"My type?" He gave me a weird look. "What . . . boys?"

"Bullies." My eyes widened. "I mean—"

Derek laughed. "Forget it. I'm not going to hurt you, Sunny."

My mouth dropped open. "You know my name?"

He nodded. "And I know you're holding auditions for a show at lunch."

Instantly, the hairs on my neck bristled. "Why? Are you going to ruin it? I know what you and your brother did to that exchange student, and I'll tell you right now, I *won't* fit in a tuba."

Bree hurried back with the napkins, and I thrust them at Derek. He just stared at me.

"Actually, I was going to try out," he said, giving me his milk carton to hold. "Unless you don't have room for big, scary bullies."

I almost dropped the carton in surprise.

"Oh! No, we do," I said. "I mean . . . anyone can try out. Sorry."

"And you won't judge me?" he asked, wiping at his shirt.

I snorted. "Well, of course I'll judge you. How else can I—"

Bree bumped me. "He means you won't *discriminate* against him?" she said under her breath.

"Oh." I blushed. "*That* kind of judging. No, I won't," I told Derek. "I promise."

"Good." He smiled and held up a pinky. "I know girls do this kind of stuff so . . ."

I grinned too, feeling silly as I hooked my pinky with the school bully's. "I pinky swear. My show is about talent, not appearance."

"That's okay, I'd do well in either category." He winked and took back his milk. "See you at noon."

I watched Derek walk away, thinking he was right. With dark hair and dark eyes . . . he wasn't bad to look at. But could he act?

Could any of them act?

• • •

I counted thirteen kids waiting outside Blakely Auditorium when Bree and I got there at lunch. They were all chatting excitedly and practicing their audition pieces for one another. When they saw me coming, they quieted and stepped to either side of the auditorium doors.

I'll admit it; I felt a bit like a superstar.

I walked past everyone and stopped before the entrance.

"Hey, guys!" I said. "So glad you could come to auditions. I want nothing but the best for this show."

Wendy, the British girl that Ilana said gestured too wildly, waved her hands over her head.

"Sorry, what *is* this show?" she asked.

"Yeah!" others chorused.

It was a good question, one even *I* didn't know the answer to. I'd moved so quickly from a one-girl show to an ensemble piece that Bree and I hadn't had time to go over scripts.

"I . . . can't release that information," I told the expectant crowd. Then in a more mysterious voice I added, "Only the ones who make the cut will know."

For something off the top of my head, I thought it was brilliant. Especially when the kids began to whisper among themselves.

"It's super-exclusive!"

"Like a secret Hollywood project!"

"Or she has no idea."

"O-kay." I clapped my hands together and pointed to the doors. "Let's get inside and get onstage!" I said.

The crowd cheered, and I braced myself against the rush of eager thespians. Thankfully, it was limited to a few shoves and one strike to my shoulder from Wendy punching me instead of the air.

"Careful, that's the director," someone told her.

"I'm an *actress*," I corrected. "I'm just selecting my costars."

But people were too busy scurrying onto the stage to notice. Bree and I settled in the front row, and a few minutes later Stefan walked in, a laptop bag hanging on one shoulder.

"Sorry I'm late," he said, giving me a hug and nodding to Bree. "I had to make some copies."

He set his bag on a chair and pulled a sheaf of packets out of the side pocket.

"Evaluation forms," he explained, handing a stack to us and keeping a few for himself. "Of course, I didn't realize there'd be this many kids trying out." He motioned to the stage with an impressed smirk.

"Neither did I," I said, counting the papers. "There's thirteen of them and fifteen packets. We'll just share."

"Sounds good," said Stefan. He pointed to a guy at the far left of the row. "Number one, you're up."

A familiar-looking dark-haired kid stepped forward and so did the one beside him. Derek! The first to step forward had been his twin brother, and they wore matching shirts. Now I knew why Derek didn't care if *his* got ruined.

Stefan groaned. "Identical twins?"

"Um . . . we just want one of you at a time," I said.

"But we have to go together. We're Guns and Ammo," said Derek's twin.

I leaned forward and furrowed my brow. "What?"

"You know, like the magazine," said Derek, looking slightly embarrassed.

I blinked at him. "I'm a thirteen-year-old girl who owns three feather boas and a rhinestoning kit. What on *earth* would make you think I know about *Guns & Ammo*?"

The brothers just stared back.

I sighed. "Okay, just . . . which of you is Guns?"

Derek blushed, rolled up his sleeve, and made a muscle with his bicep. "Ka-pow," he said.

"Oh . . . for the love of *Godspell*," said Stefan.

"I'm Ammo," Derek's brother added. Then, without

prompting, he spun around and stuck out his rear end. "And guess what I'm packing!"

"Please, no—" said Bree.

Derek's brother let fly the longest, loudest fart I'd ever heard. And of course, the excellent acoustics in the theater didn't help the situation.

Ammo and Derek high-fived, and the other boys onstage cracked up. The girls shrieked and huddled as far away as possible.

Stefan pointed at the twins and then at the door. "Out."

Ammo snickered and jumped down from the stage. "Whatever. I'm a *real* artist. Painting and sculpting beat this crap any day. Come on, Derek."

But Derek didn't budge. In fact, he looked genuinely shocked at our dismissal. "I didn't get to audition yet."

Stefan gave him a sarcastic smile. "Yes, you did . . . and it stunk."

"Thank you!" said Ammo.

"Get out!" Bree and I shouted at him.

He hurried away, but Derek stayed onstage.

"Look, I'm sorry we started with a lame joke," he said, staring right at me, "but I really do want to try out." He tugged on his shirt to straighten it. "I have a piece from . . . uh . . . *less miserables*."

Bree, Stefan, and I exchanged a glance. They both shrugged, and I wrote Derek's real name on the evaluation form with *Les Misérables* beside it.

"Go ahead," I said. "And it's pronounced 'Lay Miserahb.'"

Derek turned out to be pretty good, even doing a passable French accent. He had star potential if you overlooked his reputation and crude antics. But I wasn't sure I could. It was going to be hard enough for people to accept my show without guys like him in the cast.

Next up was Janice the spit-talker. She wasn't bad, but it was clear that her braces gave her a speech problem when it came to saying *S*s or *C*s. Every time she spoke, saliva showered forth.

"I'm Janice," she said, ending with a squirt of spit. "This (spit) piece (spit) speaks (double spit) to the actress (extra-long spit) in all of us (spit)."

Since the theater seats were several yards away, it didn't affect Bree, Stefan, or me. The stage itself, however, needed mopping by the end of her performance.

"Thank you," I said as she left the stage. "We'll be posting results this afternoon."

Stefan leaned toward me. "And will your actors be wearing wetsuits during the show?"

I shushed him and handed over Janice's evaluation for

him to fill out. "Next, please," I said, and Suresh took the stage.

Bree clapped her hands and cheered until I elbowed her.

"Thank you, *unbiased judge*," I said.

Suresh turned his back to the audience and stood with feet shoulder-width apart, arms stiff by his sides.

"Um . . . ," I said, and was interrupted by a blast of music from the sound system.

It was Michael Jackson's "Thriller."

Suresh hunched his shoulders and started to shimmy from side to side, like a zombie in the groove. The other kids started clapping to the rhythm, and Suresh spun around, dropping into a split.

"Whoa!" Bree and I said.

"Ouch!" Stefan said.

Suresh smiled at us, but when he tried to get back to his feet, the smile became a grimace. He put his hands on the floor to hoist himself up but could only scoot his entire body across the stage, still trapped in the split.

"I'm stuck!" he yelled over the music.

A couple kids dashed out and hooked him under the armpits, dragging Suresh to his feet. He looked pained but tried to find his place in the song. I waved my arms where he could see me.

Suresh gestured to someone offstage, and the music stopped.

"Don't judge me based on that," he pleaded. "I can normally get back up if I'm wearing sweatpants."

I shook my head. "That's not it. We already know you can dance. Why don't you act for us?"

Suresh stared at me, wide-eyed. "But I don't have a piece! The selection committee usually just has me dance."

That explained why he didn't get speaking roles.

"Can you borrow from someone else?" I scanned the crowd. "Derek, can you give him your script to read?"

Derek nodded and passed it over. Suresh studied it for a moment, took a deep breath, and then proceeded to use the worst French accent I'd ever heard.

"Mah nehm eez Jawn Vahl Jawn. Ah am a conveect from zee galleys."

I waved my arms again. "Lose the accent," I told him.

Suresh lowered the script. "I can't, Sunny! I'm Indian. This is the way I talk!"

I sighed and looked at Bree.

"Not *your* accent," she told him. "The French one."

Every performance that followed went a little worse. We had Wendy with the wild arms, Max the shouter, an extremely peppy girl named Holly, and Cole the stutterer, to name a few. I hated to admit it, but I could see why most of these kids hadn't been cast in a play. I was surprised they were even allowed to star in their own dreams.

Nevertheless, everyone got a round of applause as they left the theater, and I reminded them that audition results would be posted that afternoon.

When the last student left, Stefan leaned back and regarded me with raised eyebrows. "Well, *that* was entertaining, but I should get back to the high school."

"We need to pick the cast first," I said, gesturing to Bree who'd lingered in the doorway with Suresh.

"You three and Derek," said Stefan, getting up. "Call me tonight and we'll figure out a script."

"What—wait a minute!" I grabbed for his shirttail. "Who else?"

Stefan looked from me to Bree and Suresh.

"Sunny, were you watching those kids?" he asked in a low voice. "They will *not* make you look good in front of an agent."

"They couldn't have all been that bad." I scanned the evaluation forms but nobody scored higher than six out of ten. "What about Alison Brown?"

"She grunted after every line," said Stefan. "I thought she was going to drop a kidney onstage."

"But you gave her a six," I said.

Stefan shrugged. "She complimented my hair."

I sighed and kept looking, but every candidate had some obvious flaw . . . like Ilana had said. "I guess . . . maybe you're right. They're not really star material."

"Don't sound so disappointed." Stefan nudged me as he slung his laptop bag over his shoulder. "This works out better for you." He waved and headed for the exit.

I turned to Bree and Suresh with a half smile. "Welcome to our four-person show," I said.

"Sunny," Bree began, but then another voice spoke my name from the doorway.

"Sunny?" A heavyset girl with curly dark hair poked her head in. Anne Marie.

"Hey, Anne Marie, what's up?" I stood the papers on end and banged them against a chair to straighten them.

She glanced nervously at Bree and Suresh before coming forward. "Are you still holding auditions for your show?"

"Well, they're officially over." I gestured to the stage. "But you can go for it if you want."

With a grateful smile, she climbed the steps and smoothed down her skirt.

"I'll be doing a piece from *Stardust*," she said.

And as the words rolled off her tongue, she transformed

into Yvaine, the fallen star. Her voice was mesmerizing and there was no shortage of emotion in her words. When she finished, I was sad it had to end.

"Well?" she bounced up on her toes, hands clasped in front of her chest. "What do you think?"

"Honestly," I said, "I'm surprised *you're* not the lead in *Mary Pops In* instead of Sara."

Anne Marie beamed and blushed. "Well, Ilana told me I didn't fit the part." Her blush deepened. "I think she meant it literally." Anne Marie's hands outlined her round figure and settled on her stomach.

My eyes narrowed. Ilana's cruel judgment was why I'd held the auditions in the first place. I couldn't be like her. I *wouldn't* be like her.

"Ilana's an idiot," I said. "You're talented and everyone should see it. Welcome aboard."

Anne Marie's eyes outshone the stage lights. "Thank you! Thank you so much!" She bounded off the stage and shook my hand. "When do we start rehearsals?"

"Uh . . . tomorrow afternoon," I said, walking her to the exit. "And . . . don't mention this to anyone yet."

As soon as the words left my mouth, I looked into the hall and saw every person who auditioned standing there.

"Crap," I muttered.

Derek was the first to step forward.

"I'm sorry about my audition," he said. "I promise stuff like that won't happen if I'm in the play."

Cole, the boy with the stutter, joined Derek. "M-my mmmom says acting helps m-my speech."

"I really want this!" shouted Max.

Soon, everyone was talking at once, and I could see in all their faces how badly they wanted to be on that stage.

That afternoon when I posted who'd gotten into my mystery show, I didn't add a few of their names.

I added all of them.

EIGHT

YOU'D THINK SUCH A GOOD deed could only be met with cheers and offers of Chocolate Monkey muffins, but once the news was shouted through the halls, I found myself face-to-face with an angry Ilana.

"You can*not* let those kids in your show," she said.

It was the end of school and I was putting books in my locker.

"Sorry," I said, "but I don't think Your Highness rules this section of the land."

Ilana blocked my locker with her hand. "I'm serious, Sunny. You're affecting *Mary Pops In* with this."

"How?" I asked with a snort. "Are the cardboard

chimneys getting dirty without the sweeps? No villagers feeding the imaginary pigeons?"

Ilana shook her head emphatically. "Ms. Elliott wants to make both performances into a showcase, with *Mary Pops In* as the closing act. If your . . . *freak* show"—she scowled—"goes first, it could blow everything."

"That *is* a problem," I said, reaching into my locker. "But I think you've got bigger worries."

Ilana blinked in confusion. "Like what?"

I held out a pencil. "Like deciding which nostril you want this lodged in."

Ilana's face darkened. "Listen here . . ."

"No, *you* listen." I waved the pencil at her. "I get that you have diva issues no amount of red carpet can fix," I said, "but if you ever, *ever* call my cast freaks again, you will thoroughly regret it."

Even though she looked a little scared, Ilana crossed her arms and jutted out her chin. "You can threaten me all you want, but I won't let you ruin *Mary Pops In*."

"Why do you even *care*?" I asked in exasperation. "It's not like you're in the show."

Ilana smirked. "No. Of course not," she said, sauntering away. "Have a good night, Sunny. I'm off to rehearsal."

I watched her go with a curious stare. The only reason

she'd be at rehearsals was if she was in the show. But that couldn't happen unless . . .

I slammed my locker shut and hurried to Chase's. He was still there, hanging with friends before rehearsal. When he saw me, he offered a tentative smile.

"Hey, S—"

"Ilana," I cut him off. "Is she in the show?"

His very wise friends decided this was the time to leave.

"Good luck, bro," one of them said.

"She is, isn't she?" I asked.

My stomach lurched into my throat, and Chase reached for my arm, squeezing it.

"I wasn't sure how to tell you," he said. "Sara's dad got orders to transfer, so they're moving in a few months. Ms. Elliott took her out and replaced her with Ilana."

I swallowed hard. "Which means Ilana gets to be Mary Poppins, the part she wanted all along."

Chase held up a hand. "Don't read too much into this."

I gave him a disgusted look. "Ilana volunteers for the selection committee and just *happens* to get the understudy role for Mary Poppins who just *happens* to be moving in a few months. And I'm not supposed to read anything into it?"

"Sunny . . ."

I jerked my arm out of his hand. "And why are you defending her, anyway? Is she your girlfriend now?"

"What?" Chase blinked and recoiled in confusion. I couldn't blame him. I had no idea where *that* jealousy came from.

"I mean . . ." I struggled for words. "I don't care. I just thought you'd have better taste."

Chase's neck and face colored to match his hair. "Says the girl holding hands with the school bully."

"Holding ha—?" I scowled. "We were making a pinky swear, Chase!"

"Yeah, well, you've never done that with any of your other guy friends," he shot back.

"*Fine.*" I grabbed his wrist and hooked his pinky with mine. "I *swear* you are getting on my nerves!"

I wrestled my pinky free and turned away, but Chase took my hand.

"Sunny, wait. I don't want to fight anymore," he said. "We're supposed to be best friends."

I regarded him silently, taking in the hopeful smile he offered, and let out a deep sigh.

"You're right," I said, turning toward him. His hand was still on mine, and when I moved, my fingers accidentally slipped between his.

We were holding hands. It was only a matter of time before he realized it too, and freaked out.

"Uh . . ." I quickly let go and clutched my hands behind my back. "So, truce?"

"Truce," he said. "And I'm sorry for being harsh last night. It's cool that you got your own show. You'll make it awesome, I know it."

I forgot all about being embarrassed. "Awww . . . really?"

"Yes, really," he said, stepping closer.

I wanted to tell him about my mom and the agent, but my brain was turning to mush. Chase and I had stood shoulder to shoulder plenty of times but never face-to-face. My stomach was an Olympic gymnast, flipping and jumping and twirling little ribbons.

Chase was near enough now that I could see all the details of his nose and cheeks.

"You've got more freckles than usual," I said, touching one.

The muscles of his cheek moved under my fingers as he smiled even wider. "You've been counting? It's from all the sun at baseball practice."

"You should tell your dad that *sensible* young men wear sunscreen," I said in mock seriousness.

"Ha ha." Chase squeezed my fingers. "Look, sorry to give bad news and run, but I need to get to rehearsal. Can we talk later?"

I nodded. "Have fun with your . . . uh . . . girlfriend," I said, trying to sound as nonchalant as possible.

Chase laughed. "She's not my girlfriend," he said.

"Whatever," I said with a casual shrug. "Kiss her, don't kiss her . . ." I paused. "*Don't* kiss her."

He laughed again. "Good-*bye*, Sunny."

We parted ways, and I headed back to my locker. Despite the bad news of Ilana as Mary Poppins, making up with Chase made me feel worlds better. He was right—my show *was* going to be awesome, and by the end of it, I'd have an agent!

Bree had promised to meet me at my house after school, but when I rounded the block I saw both her *and* Stefan waiting on the porch. Since I'd gone against his advice and accepted everyone, I steeled myself for what was coming.

"Sunny!" Bree hurried down the sidewalk to meet me. "We've got great news."

I looked at Stefan, who was smiling just as widely.

"*Both* of you?" I asked warily. "If this is a trap, I know martial arts."

"Oh, Sunny." Stefan guided me onto the porch. "I've seen you try to kick a soccer ball and miss. You don't have the skill for martial arts."

"Fine," I said. "But you're not mad about auditions?"

He shrugged. "I wasn't thrilled when I heard your decision, but I know you've got the best intentions. And I can't argue with a good deed."

I could practically feel the halo encircling my head.

"Well," I said demurely, "I do what I can for the little people."

Stefan rolled his eyes. "All right, Saint Sunny. Let's talk about your production."

Bree stepped forward with something hidden behind her back. "We thought we could do a play that shows people you shouldn't judge a book by its cover."

My eyes widened. "I love that idea! What play?"

Bree and Stefan grinned at each other, and she whipped out the book. "Ta-da!"

"Ohhh. Neat," I said, my enthusiasm waning.

There was no way I couldn't judge this book by its cover. It had a pig on it.

Bree's face fell. "You don't like it."

I took the book from her. "No, no! I love *Charlotte's*

Web. I was just hoping for something more . . . *glamorous* than precooked bacon."

"You don't have to be Wilbur," tried Stefan. "You could be Charlotte."

"The spider? I can't spin a web with my butt." I held up a finger. "But it would be an awesome skill for my bio."

Bree held up a script. "How about *Willy Wonka*?"

"How about diabetes?" I countered. "That's what we'll get from eating so much candy."

A flicker of annoyance crossed Bree's face, and Stefan put a hand on her shoulder.

"Sunny, clearly you have something specific in mind."

He was right. I needed the agent to see the show and think "star material," not "meat is murder."

Bree held out a couple other scripts and books, but they weren't quite right. Too sad, too silly . . . one of them required me to saw a lady in half.

And then I found it.

The book had two women on the front cover. The one on the left wore a smirk on her green face as the one on the right whispered into her ear. Across the top of the book was the title "Wicked."

I gasped and held it up. "This is perfect!"

Wicked was the story of Elphaba, who later became Oz's Wicked Witch of the West, and her misunderstood school years with Galinda (aka Glinda), Good Witch of the North.

A show about a green-skinned girl facing prejudices mirrored what I was going through, what we were *all* going through, with Ilana. And even better, it was famous in the theater community.

I beamed at Stefan and Bree. "What do you think?"

Bree shuffled back and forth, as if she wanted to be excited but couldn't quite get there. "It's kind of long, isn't it?"

"We could trim it down," said Stefan, staring at the cover. "I'm sure the script is online somewhere." He glanced at me. "And for casting . . ."

"I'm Elphaba!" I raised my hand like I was in school.

"Wrong," he said. "You're Galinda."

I lowered my arm. "But . . . Elphaba's more like me."

"Then you're missing the point," said Stefan.

I frowned. "Huh?"

"Ilana says your looks don't match a famous character," said Stefan. "You need to prove that you can be the bubbly blond Galinda just the same as any white girl."

I grabbed him by the arm. "Of course!"

Bree finally clapped, startling Stefan and me. "Let's do this!"

We hurried upstairs to print out the script and spent the next couple hours arguing and assigning every role. Anne Marie had the voice and presence to play Elphaba, Suresh had the attitude for Fiyero, the lead male, Bree would make a good Nessa (Elphaba's sister) and Derek could be Boq, a supporting male.

The remaining people ended up with smaller roles, but I knew they wouldn't mind. They'd get more speaking parts and stage time than they'd ever had before.

"I can't wait for rehearsals!" I said as we assigned the last part. "Don't forget, we start tomorrow."

Stefan smiled apologetically. "I'd love to, but I've got my own performance." He slung his bag over one shoulder. "We had *Pride and Prejudice* tryouts, and I'm Mr. Darcy."

I clapped a hand to my forehead. "I forgot you were auditioning too! Congratulations!" I hugged him, partly because I was happy but also because I didn't want him to see the worried look on my face.

With Stefan in the lead role of his play, he wouldn't have time to help with mine. I'd heard horror stories from Ilana about the rigorous schedule CAA kept, and I knew that with only six weeks, my time was even shorter.

"You'll be fine," he said, as if reading my mind. "Finish cutting the script tonight, make copies, and distribute them tomorrow for a table read. Have everyone study over the weekend."

I felt like I should be taking notes. I'd never been through an entire show because extras weren't brought in until a week before opening night.

"And then?" I asked.

"And then Monday you take the stage," said Stefan.

The next morning I tracked down the cast members and handed them copies of the script with their parts highlighted. As each person saw their copy I got to share in their excitement, which was fun . . . at first.

"We're doing *Wicked*?" Wendy threw her arms open. "Brilliant!"

"Awesome!" shouted Max.

"Perfect!" said Anne Marie when I found her at lunch.

By the time I reached Derek, who was stirring pudding with a fish stick, the thrill had worn off.

"Here." I thrust the script at him. "We're doing *Wicked*. And before you say anything, I already know it's brilliant, awesome, perfect, great, and neato mosquito."

Derek glanced at the script. "You forgot one," he said.

"It's also . . . wicked." He raised an eyebrow and I couldn't help smiling.

"We're having our table read in Blakely this afternoon," I said. "Right after school."

"I'll be there," said Derek, shoving the fish stick in his mouth so he could flip through the script.

Ammo, who had been sitting beside him, frowned. "I thought you and I were gonna put open cans of tuna in the air ducts after school," he told his brother.

"You can't do that on your own?" I asked. "Or . . . not at all?"

"Mind your own business," said Ammo, pointing at me. Then, to Derek, "I need you to hoist me into the ceiling."

"I can do it *before* the table reading," said Derek. "But I can't get you back down. You'll be stuck there."

"At least you'll be at the *top* of the class," I joked.

Ammo used his fingers to pull his eyes into tight Asian slants. "Aw haw haw! You funny!" he said.

I stared at him, too shocked for a comeback.

"Stop it," Derek said, knocking Ammo's hands down. To me, he said, "Sorry. I'll see you at the reading."

I nodded and turned away as quickly as I could to hide the warmth spreading in my cheeks.

The fact that people noticed I was Asian wasn't news to

me. As far back as kindergarten, I'd been asked about my family and our background. I'd even seen people pull their eyes into slants before, but that was little kids who didn't know any better. Granted, Ammo was a flatulent idiot, but he was a year from high school, so he definitely knew right from wrong.

Even though I tried to shake the thought, it stuck with me. Who else saw me as different because I was Asian? Or Suresh because he was Indian? Or even Anne Marie because she was overweight? It was as if all this time we'd been merely tolerated, not accepted. And that bothered me. It wasn't just Ilana that my "freak" show would be speaking to, I realized. It was the whole school.

That afternoon, I shared my thoughts when everyone gathered in the theater. Well . . . almost everyone. Derek was MIA, no doubt thanks to Ammo. Most of the kids nodded quietly and a few, like Anne Marie, teared up.

"I don't want this show to focus on our differences," I said, remembering Stefan's words. "I want it to show how we're all the same. We all get scared and we all fall in love and we all laugh when something's funny."

"Like the principal stomping on his wig," someone piped up. Everyone laughed.

"And now that you know what this show is about, I

hope you still want to be a part of it and share the message," I said.

"Are you kidding? I'm in a starring role," said Suresh. "I'll share any message you want."

Several people laughed.

"Looks like we're still one person short," I said at the exact moment that Derek appeared in the doorway.

He ran down the aisle, red-faced and sweating. His hair and shirt had a gray hue to them that looked suspiciously like dust.

"Sorry . . . I'm late," he huffed. "What . . . did I . . . miss?"

"We'll talk about it later," I said with a frown. "Right now, we've got a table read to start."

NINE

I DON'T KNOW WHAT I EXPECTED from my first table read, but I was pretty sure ours was like none other . . . unless others included an argument about chickens, a bloody nose, and an arm-wrestling competition.

After my speech, everyone gathered on stage and stared in my direction expectantly. I glanced behind me, wondering who they were waiting for until I realized it was *me*.

"Oh!" I said. "Right. We don't have an official director, do we? Okay, so welcome to our first table reading," I said. "Minus the table."

Some kids laughed, and Holly the peppy girl, bounced up and down, fingers flexing above her head.

"Sunny! Sunny! Sunny!" she chirped.

"Yes, Holly," I said in my calmest voice, hoping she'd follow my example.

She didn't.

With an excited squeal she bounced forward. "For the start of the show, the munchkins sing. Do *we* get to?" She crouched with hands on knees, anxious for either my answer or the bathroom.

"Of course," I said. "I kept a few musical numbers." It dawned on me that I hadn't heard most of these kids sing. "But . . . uh . . . for now, let's just *speak* the lyrics."

"Awww," everyone moaned.

I should have let them sing. Fifteen people reciting song lyrics sounded like bored chanting. If we'd been wearing brown robes, we could have passed for monks.

Thankfully after a few verses, our narrator, Tim, was up. He had a compelling voice, but his pale skin and wide-eyed stare were a creepy combination. During auditions, one of his lines had been "I stole her heart," and with that unblinking gaze, I didn't doubt there was a shoebox of human organs under his bed.

As soon as he started narrating, Tim's eyes fixed on Cole, who was sitting across from him. After a couple minutes, Cole shifted uncomfortably and stared at the floor.

"That was good, Tim," I said. "Except maybe tone down the intensity."

"But I've got to lure the audience in," he said, regarding me with wide eyes.

"No." I resisted the urge to shudder. "No luring. You're not going to eat them. Just . . . blink more and stare less."

He looked at me and nodded, rubbing his eyes.

Then it was my turn to speak. My heart beat a little faster and the cheery voice I gave Galinda matched exactly what I was feeling. I got through about two lines before Suresh raised his hand.

"How are you going to fly down in a bubble?" he asked. "We can't afford that kind of soap."

A few people groaned.

"It wasn't a *real* bubble in the show," said Anne Marie. "It was a round cage."

"We could make one in metal shop," said Derek. "But it won't be strong enough for a person. Maybe a chicken."

"How does that help?" asked Bree. "Sunny doesn't look like a chicken."

"She might if we put a wig and a dress on it . . ."

"Guys." I halted them with a hand. "We'll worry about getting me on stage later. Let's just read." I continued with my lines, adding emotion to the song lyrics I spoke, hoping to inspire the others. But as soon as the chorus came up, the munchkins returned to their chanting. I tried to not rip my ears off as I waited for my next line.

The rest of the first scene went quickly, and thankfully, the second scene was mainly dialogue. At the end, however, Wendy got a little too exuberant and swung her arms wide.

"Owww!" said Suresh. He'd been sitting next to her but was now standing with his hands clutching his nose. A trickle of blood ran from his cupped hands down his arm.

Janice fished a Kleenex from her purse. "Use this tissue," she said, spraying saliva on it with every word.

Suresh eyed it warily. "Do I have to?"

Janice blushed but offered him a fresh one.

"Sorry, Suresh," said Wendy as he dabbed at his nose. "I got a bit carried away."

"Let me know if there are any more risky scenes," he said through pinched nostrils. "Like if you have a high kick later."

Wendy looked at her lap, and I put a hand on her shoulder.

"It's fine," I said. "Anne Marie, let's start our duet."

She nodded and our rapid back-and-forth in "What Is This Feeling?" was accompanied by the giggling of everyone around us. When the other students joined in for the chorus, this time it sounded less like chanting as they got into the scene.

Everything flowed smoothly until Bree's character admitted her attraction to Derek's character.

"Whoa, whoa, whoa!" said Suresh, waving his bloody tissue to a chorus of "Ew!"

"My girlfriend is not falling in love with anyone but me," he said.

Bree snatched the tissue away and shot him a warning look. "It's just a play, Suresh."

"I don't care. This guy isn't going anywhere near you." He gave Derek a disdainful sniff.

"Fine," I said. "Derek, do you want to switch parts with Suresh and take the lead role?"

"Whoa, whoa, whoa!" said Suresh. "Let's not get crazy. I was just making a comment." He pointed a finger at Derek. "But you better watch it, dude."

Derek just laughed. "You really want a piece of me?"

"Oooh," said the group.

Suresh got up and headed for the edge of the stage.

"Oh, come *on*!" I smacked the floor with my script.

"Suresh, don't leave!" called Bree. "He's just trying to make you mad."

"I'm not leaving," said Suresh, hopping off the stage.

"I'm going to put him in his place." He pointed at Derek. "Come here so I can do that."

I cleared my throat and gave Derek a warning glance.

He smirked at Suresh. "I'm not fighting you. It wouldn't be fair."

Suresh rolled up his right sleeve and set his elbow on the stage. "Come on. Arm wrestle me."

"Do it!" shouted Max.

Derek sighed and got up. "Fine. But so you know, I have no interest in your girlfriend." He locked his hand around Suresh's and knocked Suresh's arm backward in one motion. "There, you lost."

Suresh glanced from his fallen arm to Derek. "Best two out of three."

Everyone groaned, and Bree walked to the edge of the stage, frowning down at Suresh.

"Never mind," he said, climbing back onstage.

When Galinda and Elphaba arrived at the Emerald City, I called an end to rehearsal and reminded everyone to study their lines so we could finish the read-through the next afternoon.

"I also think we should write letters to our characters," I said.

It was an exercise from one of my acting books on

getting into character, and I thought it was a brilliant idea.

But true genius is never appreciated in its own time.

"Homework?" whined Max. "The *Mary Pops In* cast doesn't have to do this."

"Yeah, and I'm playing three different people," said Janice. "I don't want to write that many letters."

"Then just pick one," I said. "We really need to work hard if we want to impress on opening night." *Especially with an agent in the audience*, I added to myself.

The others mumbled their agreement and left the auditorium, but I asked Derek to stay and talk with me.

Hanging his head like he'd been sent to the principal, he hopped off the stage and sat in the front row.

"I said I was sorry for being late," he began before I'd even spoken.

"It's okay if you had a good reason," I said and clasped my hands in front of me. "But what were you doing that *made* you late?"

"Stuff," he said.

"Could you be more specific?"

"Things," he said.

I rolled my eyes. "Things with your brother?" I asked. "Things like climbing into vents with cans of tuna?" I pointed at the dust on one of his shoulders.

"Oh," he said. "You meant *that* specific."

I sighed. "Derek, you said you'd stop making trouble if you were in my show."

He raised an eyebrow. "And have I *brought* it to the show?" he asked.

"No," I said, "but if you get caught, it looks bad on *me* because I'm vouching for you."

Derek leaned back and crossed his arms. "Sunny, I pulled one little prank with my brother. If we get in trouble, he'll take the fall."

"Every time?" I pressed.

He groaned and stared at the ceiling. "This isn't an everyday thing. My brother just gets creative ideas and needs my help making them happen."

"His ideas aren't creative," I said. "They're destructive . . . and they make girls smell fishy so that boys won't date them." I clutched my hair to me protectively.

Derek frowned in confusion. "Huh?"

The *Mary Pops In* cast was starting to straggle into the theater, so I shook my head.

"Just . . . stay out of trouble until this show is over. Please?"

Derek threw his hands in the air. "Sure. Whatever. Can I go?"

"Yes," I said with a scowl. "Don't forget to practice your lines."

Derek gave me a sarcastic salute and marched up the aisle.

"And write the letter to your character!" I called after him.

"Fine!" he shouted back.

Chase passed Derek and glanced back curiously.

"You've upset the school bully," he said with a smirk.

I groaned and covered my face with my hands. "He'll pull the wings off some butterflies and be fine." I peeked through my fingers at Chase. "What's up with your clothes?"

He was decked out in baseball gear, cleats and all.

"I just came from practice," he said. "Why? Do I look weird?"

He actually looked cute, but that wasn't something you told your best friend.

"No," I said. "The people of London are going to be confused, though." I nodded at the *Mary Pops In* cast.

"I'll tell them it's my cricket uniform," he said with an exaggerated wink.

I smiled and bumped his shoulder with my fist. "Have fun tonight."

"I will," he said. His cheeks colored, and he ran a hand over his hair. "Hey, I had a question."

I gave him a worried look. "Everything okay?"

"Yeah. It's just . . ." He cleared his throat. "My dad gave me tomorrow night off from baseball, and we don't have show practice."

"Good!" I said with a smile. "You deserve a break."

He nodded and turned even redder. "If you want, we can go out and do something or whatever."

Go out?

I took a step back.

Chase and I had *hung* out plenty. *Going* out implied an entirely different wardrobe, diligent breath freshening, and kissing practice. Not that I was opposed to it, but—

"So?" he asked. "Do you want to hang out?"

My thoughts screeched to a halt.

Which one did he mean? Go out or hang out?

Aloud, I said, "Sounds great!" Then, hoping to get a better read on things, I added, "Where are we going on this . . . uh . . . outing?"

If he said the mall, we were hanging as friends. If he said a restaurant, we were going on a date.

"There's a new restaurant at the mall," he said. "I thought we could try it."

"That doesn't help me!" I blurted.

Chase's eyes widened.

"I mean . . . that doesn't help me decide what to *wear*," I said. "What are *you* going to wear?"

If he said jeans, we were hanging out. If he said khakis . . .

"Jeans or khakis," he said.

I wanted to punch him.

Instead, I smiled and said, "What time?"

"Six?"

"Perfect," I said. I decided to make one more effort. "How much money should I bring for dinner?"

If he made me pay, it was a friend thing. If *he* paid, it was a date.

"My dad actually has a coupon for a free meal there," said Chase.

I bowed my head in exasperation.

"Awww." He clucked his tongue and squeezed my shoulder. "Getting tired?"

I looked at him. "Incredibly so."

Before I was tempted to knock the answer out of him with a baseball bat, I said good-bye to Chase and hurried toward the exit. Ilana was waiting just outside. In the world's tiniest attempt to make amends, I gave her a passing nod.

"That rehearsal was a joke," she said to my back.

I paused and turned around. "It was a table reading," I replied. "And you were spying on us?"

Ilana leaned against a chair. "No, I was showing the finance advisor from the STARS program around, and we popped in to see the theater." She leaned closer. "If I were you, I'd shape up."

I pressed my lips together. "Or what?" I asked.

She smiled at me. "I think you've got bigger worries," she said. "Like where to find a car big enough for all your clowns."

With so many people around, she knew she could get away with that, and I knew it too. I stormed out without a word, not even noticing the guy jogging beside me until he stuttered my name.

"S-Sunny?"

I yelped in surprise, and he raised both hands.

"Sorry! I—I just wanted to talk." It was Cole, the guy I'd cast as the Wizard of Oz.

I put a hand to my chest and smiled. "It's okay. You just startled me. What's up?"

His eyes dropped to the ground. "About mmme as the wizard. I don't . . . I don't think I'm the right guy."

"What?" I frowned. "Why?"

Cole's eyes shifted to the ceiling. "It's too m-much talking. E-everyone's gonna laugh." He blinked a couple times. "You should—you should pick someone e-else."

"Uh . . . no," I said.

Cole glanced down at me in surprise. "What?"

I took his arm and pulled him over to a bench. "You wanted a speaking role to help with your stutter," I reminded him.

"I wanted a smmmall speaking role." He held up his script. "Look at all m-my lines! Like—like—like this part."

Cole then proceeded to read several lines of dialogue in a row. Almost flawlessly.

I beamed at him. "Cole, that was great!"

He chanced a small smile. "Yeah, well, m-my stutter's nnnot as bad when I—when I read or sing."

I held my arms out. "Then it's perfect that you're in a musical!"

"M-maybe," he said.

"Cole, if you mess up a couple lines, who cares?" I asked. "At least you're onstage. A lot of kids aren't even brave enough to get that far."

Cole sat up a little taller. "Yeah."

"Besides." I leaned closer. "Who's to say the Wizard of Oz *didn't* have a stutter?"

Cole grinned and got to his feet, offering me a hand up. "M-Miss Director," he said with a slight bow.

I laughed. "I'm not the director. Just an actress."

But as we said our good-byes, his comment made me think. Without a director, would the show make any progress?

I brought it up with my parents at dinner . . . though I had to word things carefully.

"Can a show be successful without a director?" I asked.

My parents glanced at each other.

"What happened to Ms. Elliott?" asked Mom.

"Did she flutter off with those fairy wings you told us about?" asked Dad with a smile.

I grinned at him. "No, Ms. Elliott's around. But she's taking a hands-off approach to the show. And I don't know if I'm . . . uh . . . *we're* . . . up to the task of running everything."

"I'm sure you're all capable," said Mom, spooning vegetables on my plate. "You've seen and been in enough productions to know what goes on."

"You just have to apply the knowledge," added Dad

"What if there's fighting?" I asked.

Mom and Dad both laughed.

"It's theater, honey. There's always fighting," said Dad. "You just have to work through your differences."

"But we don't have *time* to arm wrestle every day," I said.

Dad gave me a quizzical look. "What?"

"Don't worry," Mom told me. "Someone always steps up and takes charge. They may not *want* to, but they do it because it has to be done."

She brushed her hands together as if it were as simple as that.

But of course, nothing ever is.

TEN

BEFORE I COULD EVEN REACH my locker Friday morning, Holly bounded over on invisible springs.

"Sunny! Sunny! Sunny! Ms. Elliott wants you ASAP!"

Warning bells went off in my head. "She does? Why?"

Holly shrugged. "She just asked me to tell you."

I nodded. "Okay, thanks."

She flashed me a thumbs-up and continued to stand there, doing lunges while she watched me.

"Right now?" I asked.

Holly giggled. "I think that's the definition of ASAP."

"Okay," I said with a sigh. "Let's go."

"Want to gallop?" asked Holly. "We'll get there faster." She dashed forward a few paces and came back to me. "See?"

It was like taking a small child to the zoo.

"I'm not really in a rush to see Ms. Elliott," I said.

Holly slowed to a walk. "Why not? She's super nice."

"I know." I glanced behind us to make sure nobody was following. "But I think someone's been telling her bad things about the show."

Holly frowned. "Ilana? She can be a pain in the butt."

I busted out laughing. "Holly! I can't believe you said that!"

She looked pleased with herself.

I leaned closer. "And I can't believe you guessed right."

Holly shrugged. "People think that super peppy means super stupid, but they're wrong."

"Clearly," I said with a smile.

We stopped just outside Ms. Elliott's office, and Holly sidled up along the wall like a cat burglar.

"Do you want me to go with you?" she whispered.

I shook my head. "Thanks, but the show was my idea. I should deal with whatever happens."

"Good luck," she said solemnly. "And FYI, Ms. Elliott's prop budget got cut today."

I closed my eyes. "Great. Thanks for the warning."

Poking my head around the corner I could see Ms. Elliott stabbing numbers on her calculator and furiously scribbling on a notepad.

In the quietest voice possible, I asked, "You wanted to see me, Ms. Elliott?"

Her head whipped up so fast that her glasses slid down her nose. "Sunny!" Her smile was tight. "Sit down, please."

I perched on the edge of one of the chairs. Ms. Elliott shoved the adding machine and paper in her desk and pulled out a single piece of notebook paper with a list of names on it.

"Yours, I believe." She pushed it across the desk, and I saw it was the audition results from my show.

"Yes, ma'am," I said. "You told me if other people wanted to be in my show, I had to let them in. And I did."

Ms. Elliott leaned back. "But from what I hear, it's quite a motley crew you've got, punching each other in the face and starting fights during rehearsal."

I gritted my teeth, silently cursing Ilana.

"That punch was accidental and the fight was resolved," I said.

But Ms. Elliott wasn't listening. "I've also been told you have no director. No guidance."

"We're working on that," I said.

Ms. Elliott stood and paced the floor around me and her desk. "Sunny, when I agreed to let you do this, I trusted you'd be all right on your own."

"We will be," I said. "We just need time to get our . . . *act* together." I smiled, hoping she'd like the pun.

She didn't.

"You're not taking this seriously," she said with a frown.

"We are, I swear!" I said. "If you want, you can supervise our rehearsals."

Ms. Elliott sighed. "No, I don't have time. We've had our budget cut *after* the props were ordered, and I now have to come up with money another way." She dropped into her seat, hair gone wild and glasses crooked on her nose.

"I'm sorry that happened," I said. "But I *can* make my show work."

"I hope so," she said with a smile. "Because if I'm not impressed by your progress next Friday, I'm pulling the show."

"Next Friday?" I repeated in my most casual tone. "No problem."

"Good." Ms. Elliott returned to her calculations and I backed out gracefully.

But the second I reached the hallway, not even a cheetah could've outrun me.

"Breeeeee!" I shouted when I tracked her down in the math lab.

She looked up from her notebook with wide eyes. "I'm working on the letter to myself right now, I swear!"

"No, it's not you. It's Ilana!" I growled.

Bree dropped her pencil. "Oh no. Is it something with the show? Is it canceled?"

"It will be if we can't impress Ms. Elliott by next Friday," I said.

Bree's skin turned paler than her paper. "How impressive do we have to be?"

"Level Two impressive," I said.

"Level Two." She swallowed audibly and put her notebook away. "What do you need?"

"Meet me in the cafeteria at lunchtime. Spread the word to the rest of the theater group . . ." I held up a finger and corrected myself. "*Our* theater group." I rubbed my chin. "We should really come up with a name. Like 'Broadway Bound' or 'The Talent Troupe.'"

Bree grabbed my arm. "Sunny."

"Right. Focus. I'll see who else I can track down. And don't breathe a word to anyone outside the . . . group." Then I darted out of the room.

I was able to get the message to five other people before

lunch, and when I reached the cafeteria, I was pleased to see that word had spread to everyone. They were all sitting at a corner table in the art crowd, whispering nervously and glancing around.

Bree was the first to spot me and wave me over.

"We figured this was the best place to sit," she said, "since artists and actors don't really get together and gossip."

"Good idea," I said, unrolling a large piece of paper and taping it to the table. To the rest of the group I said, "Guys, we have a little problem. Ms. Elliott heard how bad our first reading went—"

"I thought it was great," interrupted Suresh.

Bree turned to him. "Really? Was that before or *after* the arm wrestling?"

"*Anyway*," I said. "She's afraid we're not taking this seriously, so next Friday she's going to evaluate us. We've got to be up to Level Two standards."

Bree nodded, and Suresh and a few others groaned.

Anne Marie raised her hand. "What's Level Two?"

I held up a black marker. "Good question." On the giant sheet of paper I wrote the numbers one through seven. Then I wrote the following:

1: Lines

2: Songs

3: Memory

4: Costumes and props

5: Blocking and lights

6: Dress rehearsal

7: Performance

"According to friends of mine, every CAA theater production has seven levels to completion," I said. "One for each week. Level One is reading lines." I underlined the word.

"That means by the end of the first week there can't be any mispronunciations or hesitation," said Bree.

"But we've had only one table reading," Wendy spoke up. "And, as Sunny says, it stunk."

I pointed my marker at her. "That's why we're in trouble. Next week when Ms. Elliott comes, we should be done with line reading and have our musical numbers down."

My words were met with a chorus of groans.

"If we can't produce," I said, "Ms. Elliott cancels the show."

The groans turned to wails of despair.

"We'll never make it!" shouted Max.

"It's impossible!" said Wendy, pounding the table with her fists.

I glanced at Bree. "Maybe our group name should be 'The Melodramatics.'"

She grinned. "I actually kind of like that."

Thankfully, among all the moans and groans there were a few voices of optimism.

"We just have to work harder," said Anne Marie.

"Until there's blood, sweat, and tears!" agreed Tim, eyes wider than ever.

A couple kids shifted uncomfortably.

I squeezed Tim's shoulder. "I like your enthusiasm, but let's leave out bodily fluids." To the others, I said, "Guys, it'll be easy. If we meet this weekend, we can practice five or six times and be back on schedule for Level Two on Monday!"

Again, my bright idea was underappreciated.

"You want me to give up my weekend for this?!"

"Saturday and Sunday are my only days *away* from school!"

"I have to help my brother put red dye in the park fountain so it looks like blood!"

The last one was, of course, from Derek.

I was close to having a riot on my hands, but I

remembered what my mom had said the night before.

Someone always steps up and takes charge.

I didn't want the role of director, but I was the closest we were going to get. So I listened for a minute more to the complaints and took a steadying breath.

"Guys," I said, "I'm sorry to take your personal time, but it's one Saturday afternoon. I'll give you today off, and we can read at the park tomorrow so you won't have to come to school." I turned to Derek. "And so *you* can watch your brother get handcuffed when the cops bust him."

People still didn't seem convinced.

It was time to pull out all the stops.

"All right, listen." I leaned closer and lowered my voice. "You guys have to keep this a secret, but on opening night, there's going to be an agent in the audience."

At the mention of an agent, the mood at the table instantly shifted. Instead of slumping over in dejection, everyone sat up a bit straighter with a new fire in their eyes. Of course, none of them knew the agent was only coming to see me.

But as long as it motivated them, what could it hurt?

"What do you say, guys?" I asked. "A few days ago you had nothing. Now you've got a chance at fame."

"I'm in," said Suresh, holding up his hand.

Bree beamed at him. "Me too." She held up her hand.

Mine went up, as did Anne Marie's and a couple others. Slowly, every other hand raised except for Derek's.

"Come on," I told him. "Just a few hours."

He sighed. "My brother's going to kill me." But he finally raised his hand.

"Excellent!" I cheered. "See you guys tomorrow at one o'clock in the park!"

They all dispersed to grab food and visit other friends. All of them except Derek.

"So . . ." He shoved his hands in his back pockets. "Since I agreed to hang out with you guys instead of my brother—"

I smiled. "You're not in trouble anymore, Derek."

"Good," he said, relaxing a little. "Oh. And here." He pulled a folded piece of paper from his back pocket.

"What's this?" I asked.

I started to open it, but Derek stopped me.

"Don't read it here. It's the letter to my character," he said.

I stared at the paper, which suddenly felt different in my hand. Like it was more than just lead on a page.

"Derek, I'm . . . impressed," I said with a smile. "You didn't turn in a blank sheet like Suresh."

Derek smirked. "Suresh handed in a blank sheet?"

I nodded. "He said his character spends so much time goofing off in class, he probably can't read anyway."

Derek laughed. "I should've thought of that!"

"Well . . . thanks for the letter," I said. "And sorry to pull you away from all the fun you had planned."

He shrugged. "My brother has his art. It's time for me to have my own thing too."

We waved good-bye, and I smiled to myself until I turned and bumped into . . . his evil twin.

"Hey," I mumbled, stepping around him.

"Hey," said Ammo. He held out a rolled-up piece of paper. "Listen, I wanted to offer this as my way of saying sorry for the other day. I didn't mean to single you out with that insult."

"Really?"

This was turning into a *very* surprising lunch period.

"Wow, thanks, Ammo!" I unrolled the paper. "You didn't have to—"

The words "Freak Show" glared up at me, scribbled in black marker.

That was more what I expected.

Ammo tapped the paper. "I overheard Ilana say that and thought it was catchy."

Below the title he'd drawn caricatures of everyone in my cast with their flaws amplified. Max had an enormous mouth; Wendy's arms were long, wiggly, and out of control; Janice was a fountain spewing saliva . . . and standing apart from all of us was Derek, bound and gagged.

I crumpled the paper and shoved it in Ammo's chest.

"*You're* a jerk!" I snapped.

Ammo shrugged. "I told you I didn't mean to single you out. I meant to insult *all* of you." He uncrumpled the paper and pointed to an illustration. "Look at the one of you. I didn't know whether to go with ruthless dictator or Bruce Lee." He shrugged. "I wasn't sure if you knew any martial arts."

I smiled sweetly at him. "I know *one* kick."

It wasn't a move Bruce Lee would've approved of, but it definitely brought Ammo to his knees.

ELEVEN

"MY LITTLE GIRL IS GOING on her first date!" cooed Mom that afternoon. Her reflection hovered behind mine in the mirror while I got ready to meet Chase.

"It's not a *date*," I told her. "We haven't called it that, and he hasn't given me any cattle."

"I see." Mom pulled my hair back and twisted it on top of my head. "Well, if it's not a date, I guess you won't want *that*." She nodded to a white box on the bathroom counter.

"What is it?" I tried to sound casual, but my fingers fumbled to get it open. Dark purple gemstones twinkled at me.

I sucked in my breath and lifted one of the earrings out of the box. "They're gorgeous."

"Purple sapphires," said Mom, shielding my eyes from a hairspray shower. "From one of my movies. The director let me keep them."

"Wow," I said. "The only thing *I* ever got from a show was a *Peter & the Pans* poster."

Mom gave me a curious look.

"From that kindergarten play I did where Peter Pan grows up to be a dessert chef?" I reminded her.

She nodded. "That's right. You were one of the Lost Boysenberries." We smiled at each other in the mirror.

"Lame," I said. "But it was my ticket to stardom, right?"

Mom squeezed my shoulder. "You're still young. And look how far you've already come! Star of the school play with a potential *agent* in your future!" She winked at me.

I lowered my head and stared at the sapphires.

"About that—" I ventured.

"Try the earrings," she said. "Let's see how they look."

Since they were beautiful in the box, I knew they'd be just as pretty in person. And sure enough, with my hair pulled up, I looked like the movie star I wanted to be instead of the fraud I actually was.

"Perfect!" Mom clapped her hands together.

"Mom," I said. "There's—"

She held up a finger. "I think I hear something."

Dad poked his head in the bathroom. "Chase is waiting downstairs, ladies." He stepped back and smiled at me. "Your first date."

My eyes widened, and I put my finger to my lips. "Dad, shhh! It's not a date!" I whispered.

Dad glanced over his shoulder and turned back with a smile. "The way he's dressed, I'd have to disagree."

"What?!" Sweat sprang up on my palms, and I gave Mom a worried glance.

"You look beautiful," she promised, pushing me toward the staircase.

"How is he dressed?" I asked Dad, clinging to the banister. "Business suit? Tuxedo? Did he bring a marriage cow?"

"*Go*," said Dad, prying up my fingers. "Have fun. But be home by nine."

I patted my hair and ran my hands down my blouse, leaving sweat streaks behind. My earrings were classy, but the rest of me screamed *Awkward!*

Chase was sitting in the front room, and he stood when he saw me. He was wearing jeans too (thank goodness) but had definitely stepped up his shirt from the usual hang-out attire. He even smelled nicer.

"Hey, Sunny," he said. "You look—"

"I just washed my hands!" I blurted in greeting. "And I used my shirt to dry them!" I pointed to the sweat streaks.

"Uh . . . same here," he said, pointing to identical stains on his button-up.

Our eyes met, and we laughed.

"So . . . you look good," I said, ducking my head in embarrassment.

"Thanks." Chase blushed. "My dad thought I was underdressed." He lowered his voice an octave in his best imitation. "Nothing says 'successful bachelor' like a coat and tie!"

"Bachelor?" I repeated. "He knows you're thirteen, right?"

"Going on thirty," said Chase with a nod. "And . . . um . . . I was going to say that you look nice too, also, by the way."

I blushed and moved to wipe sweat on my clothes again, but thought better of it and put my hands behind my back.

"Ready to go?" I asked.

Chase cleared his throat and held open the front door. "Fair lady." He bowed with a sweeping gesture.

I laughed, glad to be back in our comfort zone. With a

curtsy, I stepped onto the porch and glanced up and down the street.

"Where is the chariot to take us to yonder shopping mall?" I asked.

"Alas," said Chase, "we journey on foot, for my father believes it builds character."

"And blisters," I said.

But it was a cool night, and I couldn't have had better company. The entire walk there, we sang show tunes from our favorite musicals. Mine was *Singin' in the Rain* and Chase's was, of course, a musical about baseball called *Damn Yankees*.

Just for him, I launched into a rendition of "Shoeless Joe from Hannibal, MO." Chase whistled and clapped.

"Much better than the high school production," he said.

"Be nice!" I nudged him. "Stefan was in that."

"And Stefan was good," Chase said loyally. "But the girl playing the reporter sounded nothing like you."

I blushed and grinned. "Thanks."

Dinner was delicious, but I still wasn't clear whether or not we were on a date. Chase held the door open for me when we walked into the restaurant, but he also burped while drinking soda. He paid to split a dessert with me, but he also ate more than half.

Truthfully, though, it didn't matter. I was with my best friend, laughing about school production nightmares and talking about the agent coming to my show. If it never turned into anything more, it was still a great night.

On the way home we walked side by side in silence. Chase drifted a little closer with every step until our hands were bumping. Then, without a word, he turned his wrist and entwined his fingers with mine.

"Ahhh *ha*!" I shouted so loud he jumped several feet.

"Geez, Sunny!" Chase put a hand over his heart. "What was that for?"

"This *was* a date!" I exclaimed in triumph.

Chase pulled his hand away from his chest and ran it through his hair. "Well, yeah," he said with a shy smile. "Is that okay?"

"Of course," I said, offering him my hand.

He reached for it cautiously. "Are you going to scream again?" he asked.

I stuck out my tongue and placed our hands together.

"You shouldn't call this hanging out, by the way," I said. "It's very confusing."

Chase nodded. "Got it. When do you want to *go out* next?" he asked.

"Thank you," I said with an approving nod. "And is tomorrow night too soon? That was a good restaurant."

Chase laughed. "I'd totally go back, but I've got baseball *and* theater practice. How about lunch somewhere tomorrow afternoon?"

"That's when *I* have theater practice," I said. "As long as the rest of the Melodramatics show up."

"The Melodramatics?" Chase repeated with a grin.

"I meant it to be funny, but I kinda like it now," I said.

"Me too," said Chase. "It definitely fits you."

"Hey!" I pushed him.

We reached my front porch and sat on the swing.

"Baseball *and* theater in one night," I said. "So you're starting with the fun stuff that makes you feel alive . . . and then going to baseball?"

Chase didn't laugh. "I don't mind it. I just hate that it's supposed to be a punishment for wanting to do theater." He stared at his hands. "My dad almost didn't let me in the show this year, you know."

I shook my head. "Sorry he's such a jerk."

"He's not *all* bad," said Chase. "It's just . . . after my mom died, he lost touch with anything creative. I think her cancer made him take everything too seriously."

I reached for Chase's hand and held it. He didn't talk about his mom much, even though she'd been the one who got him into acting.

"Sorry," I said again.

"It was fun while it lasted," Chase said with a shrug. "But I suppose I have to grow up sometime."

"Don't say that," I said. "I don't want to date an old man."

Chase grinned. "I should probably go. It's getting late . . . and your parents are watching us from the living room."

"What?" I spun around in time to see the window blinds snap closed.

I rolled my eyes at Chase. "Sorry *again*."

"Me too," he said.

We both sat there awkwardly for a second, knowing what came next. The good night kiss.

"So . . . ," said Chase, rubbing his hands over his knees.

"Don't take this the wrong way," I said. "But I'm not ready."

"Oh, good." His whole body relaxed. "Me neither." Chase lifted my hand and kissed the back of it. "But thank you for an awesome evening."

I couldn't help giggling. "You're welcome."

He hopped off the swing and took the porch steps two at a time.

"Bye!" I called down. "Have a good night!"

"Already there," he said with a grin.

Saturday's read-through at the park was way less eventful than Thursday's, with the only trouble when we first arrived at the picnic tables. I'd reserved a special section but was surprised to see a folded, handwritten place card waiting at every seat.

"These are nice," said Bree, picking hers up.

"No, they aren't," said Anne Marie. "Read what's inside." She held hers up for my inspection.

"Why was the elephant covered in barbecue sauce?" I read. "Because Anne Marie couldn't find ketchup."

The rest of us flipped ours open, and the muttering and yelling began. Mine said, "How are Sunny and fortune cookies the same? They're both Asian and full of useless information."

"Who would write all these mean things?" asked Holly.

I glanced at Derek. He put his place card behind his back, but not before I noticed it was blank inside.

"Throw them away," I told the others, "and let's get to work."

That night, I went with my parents and Grandma to the latest theater production in town. They saw it as a reward for me landing a stellar role, but I saw it as research. Granted, I felt a little guilty taking advantage of their confusion about what play I was in, but I was doing this for the team.

My eyes never left the actors during the performance, and when Dad asked if I wanted to stretch my legs at intermission, I declined. Instead I spent the downtime eyeing the lights and jotting notes in my playbill about things I'd seen onstage.

"Don't forget scene transitions," Grandma said in a low voice.

I nodded and continued to scribble furiously.

Mom, who sat on Grandma's other side, leaned over. "Are you enjoying the show or working?" she asked.

I glanced up and smiled. "Both. Monday we start music number rehearsals."

"Ooh. Wonderful!" Mom rubbed her hands together. "Professional orchestra or student?"

"Huh?" I furrowed my brow.

"Who's performing your songs?" she asked.

My pencil lead snapped against the page. I'd completely forgotten to think about who'd actually provide the music.

"It's a student orchestra," Grandma spoke up, giving

me a meaningful look. "They've got a nice pianist."

Mom nodded. "Jesse, right?"

"Why . . . yes." Grandma nodded. "Such a pretty—"

"Jesse's a boy," I whispered.

"Pair of hands he has," Grandma finished.

Mom gave her a funny look. "Yes, I suppose so."

Grandma smiled indulgently at Mom before giving me a double eyebrow raise.

"I know, I know," I mumbled, jotting two words on my playbill.

Get orchestra.

Monday morning I was at school bright and early again. My hope was to find somebody, anybody, in the music room who I could coax into being part of my orchestra for the show. As luck would have it, I found *several* students tuning their instruments when I walked in.

"Hey, sounding good!" I said.

A guy with a cello regarded me suspiciously. "Do you really know or are you just saying that?"

"I know the important stuff," I said with a confident smile. "Do-Re-Mi. La-Ti-Do." My mind went blank. "*I* before *E* except after *C*."

The guy didn't look impressed. "Why are you gracing us with your musical talent?"

"Oh! Well, I was wondering if you might be free to play a show in a few weeks," I said, crossing my fingers.

"You mean *Mary Pops In*?" An Asian girl with a violin strolled over. Her features were more pronounced than mine, and I wondered if anyone ever made slant eyes at her. "Why do you think we're practicing?"

My face fell. "You're playing the spring show?"

"Of course," said the girl. "What were *you* talking about?"

I shook my head. "Is there anyone in the music department who *isn't*?"

"Sorry," said the girl. "We're all booked up."

"I don't suppose you'd consider performing for two shows . . . ," I said hopefully. "Mine goes on right before."

The cello player leaned over his music stand and showed me a piece of paper. "This is the song list we have to perform. What do you think?"

My shoulders drooped. "Well, thanks anyway." I paused and looked at the Asian violinist. "Can I ask you something personal? Do you ever get left out of concerts because you're . . ." I gestured to her face. "You know."

"Not wearing makeup?" she asked.

"No." I leaned in and whispered, "Asian. Like, do they ever pick another kid to play instead of you?"

The violin player looked at the cello player and they both laughed.

"Are you joking?" asked the cello player. "She's every orchestra's dream. That automatically puts her in first chair."

I stared at him, perplexed. "Why?"

"Because I'm an Asian violinist," said the girl. "Everyone wants one."

I continued to draw a blank. "Again, why?"

"They're musically gifted," the cello player said simply.

That was the logic?

Ilana wouldn't pick an Asian girl for an acting role because of her race, but the orchestra would favor an Asian girl for the same reason. I'd never considered the possibility that discrimination could go both ways.

Grandma was right; *everyone* judged.

My brain was starting to hurt from so many deep thoughts, and I was no closer to having my music. At lunchtime, I confided my dilemma in Bree, but she didn't share my concern.

"If we don't have an orchestra, we don't have it," she said with a shrug. "An iPod is cheesy, but we'll make it work."

"But I don't even know if most of these kids can sing!" I said.

Bree grabbed a carton of milk. "I've got choral group with Holly, Anne Marie, Tim, and Max, so I know they're pretty good," she said. "The ones that aren't, we'll ask to sing solo."

I raised my eyebrow. "Solo?"

"Yeah. 'So low' we can't hear them."

We both snickered.

But it wasn't as funny at rehearsal that afternoon.

On Saturday I'd told everyone to listen to the six songs we were going to do and practice them over the weekend. On Monday it sounded like everyone had listened to the sound of cats fighting and practiced that instead.

I tried not to wince as we got through the first verse of the opening song. But on a particularly high note my eye started twitching and I had to cut off the iPod.

"Okay," I said. "We have work to do."

"Already?" asked Anne Marie. "We've only been singing for two minutes."

"Two minutes longer than we should have," said Suresh. "I agree with Sunny. We suck."

Some people booed but others nodded.

"Let's take it in smaller groups," I said. "Everyone that sings soprano on this side of the stage, tenors over there." I pointed to the other side.

Most of the boys migrated across the stage and I had the remaining sopranos stand in a line.

"Let's take it from the top," I said, pressing play on the iPod.

They belted out the lyrics, sounding only half as off-key. Then again, there were only half as many of them. But someone was still killing the high notes.

I walked from person to person, listening as they sang. When I reached Derek, I stopped.

"Good neeeews!" he trilled like a whistle.

I turned off the iPod. "Derek, that's really impressive, but it's also *really* high."

He puffed out his chest as if I'd given him a compliment. "I was in falsetto choir at church."

"Back when you were a little girl?" asked Suresh.

Derek sneered at him. "Who could still beat you at arm wrestling."

"You wanna go?" Suresh started forward, but I stopped him.

"Derek, falsetto choir is impressive, but the good news we're singing about has to do with the Wicked Witch, not Jesus," I said. "Why don't we lower it an octave?" I suggested.

Derek tried again. The other sopranos joined in and

this time the voices blended much better. I switched to the tenors.

"Show me what you've got," I said.

For a voice range that came closer to natural conversation, I thought the guys would have nailed it. But the end result was all over the place.

"Try this pitch," I said, lowering my voice. "Ahhh."

A few of them were spot-on and the rest were only slightly below or above. But there was something missing . . . a voice that hadn't joined in.

I walked around the group again, stopping at Suresh. When he realized I was watching, his throat muscles moved, and forced out the worst sound known to man.

"Aughhh!"

My eyes involuntarily widened, but I tried to give him the benefit of the doubt. Maybe the other voices had affected his.

"Let me hear just Suresh," I said.

"Aughhh!" he sang, like a tortured man in a haunted house.

I looked to Bree and she just rubbed her forehead.

The other guys tried to help Suresh, but he still sounded as if a guy with a hook hand was chasing him.

"Aughhh!"

I clapped my hands. "Let's work on that later. Suresh, for now, just . . . go back to what you were doing," I said.

He blushed and disappeared into the back of the group.

"Sopranos, sing high," I continued, "but not too high, and tenors sing lower."

I started the music, and this time our group created a tolerable sound. If we practiced hard, we wouldn't embarrass ourselves in front of Ms. Elliott. Although Suresh might be a different case.

When everyone took a break to get water, I pulled Bree aside.

"So, your boyfriend," I said, trying to think of a tactful way to approach the issue. "He takes singing to an entirely different place."

"Does he?" asked Bree, looking everywhere but at me. "I never noticed. I guess love makes you blind."

"Yeah, *blind*. Not deaf," I said. "You can't tell me you don't hear that. A knife scraping a plate sounds better."

"All right, he's awful!" Bree said, running a hand through her hair. "But since he's such a good dancer, we figured that would make up for it."

"Not unless he's in space, where no one can hear him scream!" I said. "Bree, we have an agent to impress!"

I couldn't sing opposite Suresh's screeching. The agent

would have her fingers in her ears, and she'd never hear *my* voice.

Bree wrung her hands together. "What can we do?"

"I don't know. How's he gotten by all this time?" I asked.

Bree gazed sadly at Suresh. "Usually, he sings softly in the background. And at parties, people have him just mouth the lyrics to 'Happy Birthday.'"

"Well, he's the male lead so he can't mouth the lyrics," I said.

No sooner had I said it than a thought struck me. From the way Bree's eyes brightened, I could tell she had the same idea.

"Or can he?" I whispered. "We can pull a *Singin' in the Rain*. We'll record someone else singing and use *that* while Suresh lip-synchs along!"

"But who would do his vocals?" she asked.

"Someone in the *Mary Pops In* cast," I said. "We'll just have to sit in on a practice and pick the best one."

"How?" asked Bree. "Their practices are only open to the stars."

I pointed overhead to the control booth.

"We'll listen from in there. Tomorrow afternoon, we commence with Operation Golden Voice," I said.

TWELVE

SPYING ON THE *MARY POPS In* cast wasn't just a good idea for Operation Golden Voice; it was a great way to see what a real rehearsal looked like from beginning to end.

I continued our music practice as planned but sent everyone home ten minutes early.

"Great job on those letters to your characters," I said. "For tonight's exercise, I want you to *eat* like your character."

Everyone liked that idea . . . except Max.

"My character's a goat!" he cried.

"Come on," said Derek, guiding him toward the door.

"I'll drink a soda, and you can eat the can."

While everyone left, I lingered behind with Bree. Our excuse was that we were checking the acoustics from various spots in the theater, and I made my way toward the control booth with Bree belting "Dancing Through Life" from the stage.

When the last cast member left, I sprinted the remaining distance to the control booth and slipped inside. The back of the booth had sound equipment and a door leading to the rear entrance of the theater. The front of the booth was floor-to-ceiling tinted glass, where I could see Bree dashing up the aisle toward me.

"I thought they'd never leave!" she said.

She closed the side door and shuffled forward. With the lights off and the windows tinted, it was pretty dark. I held out my hand and guided her to the control table where I was sitting. "This is so exciting!"

"I know!" she whispered back. "Like we're on stakeout!"

Bree settled into a chair, and I glanced at a digital clock on the table. Ten minutes until *Mary Pops In* took the stage.

"Hey, Sunny?" Bree nudged me. I couldn't see her in the darkness, but I turned to face her anyway.

"What's up?" I asked.

"I've been meaning to tell you . . ." Her voice took on a

shy tone. "Thanks for letting me in your show. I know you wanted to be on your own—"

"It's better like this," I interrupted. "By myself, I'd look like a dork. With others, I'll look like one of many dorks."

Bree laughed. "I'm serious. Nobody else would have given me this chance, and maybe nobody will again."

I felt for her arm in the dark. "Don't say that. You're good."

"But not loud," she said. "And that's what directors want."

I snorted. "Uh . . . microphones were invented for a reason. If your only problem is that you can't bust someone's eardrums—and that *is* your only problem, by the way—you've got nothing to worry about."

Bree shifted in her seat. "You're sweet to say that. Do you think the agent will notice?"

My skin prickled, and I was grateful Bree couldn't see the guilty look on my face.

"If you give it your very best, I don't see why not," I said.

Thankfully, that answer seemed to satisfy Bree. A few moments later, the theater doors swung open, and Ilana burst in with several other actors on her heels.

"Here we go," I whispered.

A small thrill went up my spine as I saw Chase walk in with a couple buddies, and I resisted the urge to knock on the glass and wave to him. Or rather . . . Bree made me resist the urge.

"Don't draw any attention," she warned. "Ilana would eat us alive."

I glanced at the stage. "You mean like those kids in the corner?"

Ilana had backed two chimney sweeps against a wall and was scolding them.

"I wish I could hear her," said Bree.

"She's probably saying 'If any of that dust gets on me, I'm gonna kick you in the chim-chimi-knee!'" I guessed.

Bree snickered. "And they're saying 'Soot yourself!'"

I put my hand over my mouth to keep the laughter in. Luckily for the chimney sweeps, Ilana was intent on starting the rehearsal, and she darted about the stage snapping at people and herding them into the center.

"She's like a sheepdog," said Bree.

"Except sheepdogs don't bite as hard," I said.

Everyone gathered in a large circle, but instead of instructing like I expected, Ilana joined the circle too.

"What are they doing?" I asked.

Before Bree could answer, Chase stepped into the middle

of the circle and stopped with his arms outstretched.

"I am a telephone pole," he said in a loud, booming voice.

Someone from the opposite side of the circle stepped in and held onto one of Chase's arms.

"I am a bird on a telephone pole," she proclaimed.

"They must be doing a warm-up exercise," I whispered. "That's a good idea."

"Um . . . no," said Bree. "I'm not hanging from someone's arm and making bird calls."

A boy joined the two in the middle. "I am a man shooting a bird on a telephone pole," he said.

"Not even if someone would put you out of your misery?" I asked Bree.

She giggled and whispered, "Shhh."

The warm-up continued until Ilana was the last person to join. When she finished, everyone clapped and ran off stage.

Those who weren't in the opening scene sat in the audience, except for two guys who, to my horror, headed straight for the control booth.

"Crap!" I whispered. "Abort mission, Bree!"

"What do we do?!" she squeaked.

"Out the back!"

We ran for the exit. I turned the knob, but the door wouldn't budge. "It's locked from the inside!"

"Sunny," said Bree, "*we're* on the inside."

"Oh. Right!" I ran my hand up and down the frame, feeling for a deadbolt. I unlatched it and pushed with all my might. Nothing.

"Sunny, they're almost here!" Bree warned.

"It's stuck!" I hissed at her.

"Too late!" Bree tugged me away from the door and back to the table. "Hide!"

We cowered underneath and formed our bodies into the tiniest balls possible. The light from the outside hallway revealed two pairs of feet advancing on us. I squeezed Bree's hand, but thankfully, the owners of the feet just dropped into chairs.

"I am *so* done with this theater crap," one of the guys said. "Wait, that's not right. I'm so done with *Ilana's* crap."

"No joke," said the other guy. "Control freak to the extreme."

I wished they'd shut up so I could hear what was happening onstage. Chase was the first to appear, and the guys at the table cued his music.

Chase sang well, but there was no arrogance in his voice, which was what I needed for Fiyero. The rest of the villagers crowded around to listen to Chase singing poetry in the park while playing a bongo drum.

The intro song ended, and he and the villagers left. The scene changed to Mrs. Banks and her followers, the Soul Sister Suffragettes, vying for gender equality. They sang:

We're clearly soldiers in flashy tights.

Dauntless crusaders for womens' rights

I bit my hand to keep a giggle from escaping, especially when they got to the chorus.

Our daughters' daughters will applaud us

Saying "Y'all are just the hottest!"

You rock, Soul Sister Suffragette!

Bree shifted beside me, and I heard her let out a soft whimper of laughter.

But then something strange happened. The longer I watched, the more I noticed how professional and put-together the cast was. They moved seamlessly from song to song, and their voices blended in harmony. Forget needing a week's worth of practice; they were ready to go.

Bree nudged me as a guy named Cam stepped onstage and started singing. He was playing Mr. Banks, so parts of his lines were spoken, but the rest he warbled in a throaty voice that had just a hint of conceit.

Cam's pipes were perfect for Fiyero.

All I needed was to coax him into recording Suresh's singing parts and then practice like mad with the others to get their numbers nailed down by Friday.

But that would have to wait until I tackled a bigger, more immediate problem.

The guys manning the control booth were getting bored. And when guys get bored, disgusting things happen.

"Hey," one of them said, "guess what I ate for lunch."

The other one chuckled. "What?"

In answer, his friend farted long and loud.

Both guys cracked up.

"Ugh, dude, I'm guessing you ate spoiled eggs!" the non-farter said.

Bree stiffened beside me, and I tried to maintain my cool. Maybe farts worked on the same principle as hot air. Maybe they rose into the atmosphere, and we'd be safe under the table.

"Dude. Check this out," said the non-farter. And then he quickly lost *that* title, releasing his own.

I was wrong. I was ever so wrong! Farts didn't work like hot air. Farts worked like sprinklers, hitting everything in a twelve-foot radius. I clamped my hand over my nose and got as close to the floor as possible, hoping the worst was over.

But *everything* was a contest with guys.

"Oh yeah?" said the one who'd first let fly. "How about—"

"Stop!" I popped my head out from under the table, and both guys screamed. One of them fell out of his chair entirely. "It's like a gas chamber in here!"

"Yeah," said Bree, popping out to join me. The guys screamed again. "Why don't you clip an air freshener to the back of your pants?"

"What . . . what are you doing here?" one of them asked, flipping on the light. Bree and I looked at each other.

"We were . . . taking a nap," I said. "Until you disturbed us."

Bree shook her head. "Looks like we'll have to find someplace else to go." She brushed past the boys and pulled open the door on the back wall.

"Oh, it's a *pull*," I said.

She silenced me with a look, and we walked with quiet dignity out the exit. Once we were in the hallway, though, we burst into giggles.

"That was *nasty*!" I said, doing a shudder dance.

"They could definitely take Ammo in a battle of the butts," said Bree.

We fell against the wall, laughing, until we heard footsteps clomping down the hall, swift and determined.

Bree paled and her eyes widened. "The principal?"

I set my lips in a tight line, recognizing the footfalls. "Someone even worse," I said. "Chase's dad."

A tall, red-haired man in a snappy black suit and tie came around the corner. He smiled broadly when he saw us.

"Good evening, ladies! Sunny, have you seen Chase?" He stuck out his arm and tapped his watch. "He's a little late for baseball practice."

I peeked into the auditorium. "He's onstage, Mr. O'Malley. Doing the chimney sweep waltz."

Mr. O'Malley's eyebrows lifted. "He's a chimney sweep . . . and a dancer? *Those* sound like promising career paths."

He smiled again, but his neck muscles were tight.

"It's just a play, sir," I said. "I'm sure he's got big dreams for his future. Big . . . *responsible* dreams."

"Well, he's not going to see them come true if he's dancing with brooms." Mr. O'Malley bent to eye level with me. "Be a doll and fetch him, won't you?"

I stepped back and held the door open. "Parents are allowed in, sir."

"Yes, well, I'd rather not be sucked into"—he waved his arm in front of him—"that nonsense." He reached into his pocket and pulled out a phone, punching unseen keys on its surface.

"I'll go," said Bree, slipping past me into the theater. She could probably feel the tension building between me and Mr. O'Malley.

"Sir," I said, leaning against the wall, "if you're so against this, why do you even let Chase stay at CAA?"

Mr. O'Malley shifted his eyes to look at me without lifting his head.

"His mother wished it, and I'm not one to dishonor her memory," he said. He went back to looking at his phone. "Besides, his education here's almost over. When he reaches high school, he'll put theater behind him."

"But what if he doesn't want to?" I asked.

Mr. O'Malley winked at me. "He wants to."

I pressed my lips together, wondering how much further I could push it. "He seems to be really good at it."

"Oh, I know he is," Mr. O'Malley admitted. "In fact, I don't think there's anything that boy of mine *can't* do well." He puffed out his chest a bit.

Chase was right. He wasn't all bad.

"You should see his trophy collection," his dad continued.

"His mother made me promise to keep every one. Even his Best Supporting Goat ribbon for *Three Billy Goats Gruff*." His shoulders shifted as he chuckled to himself.

"Really?" I asked with a smile.

He nodded. "She wanted him to remember that life rewards you for working hard." His face softened a little. "She was a smart woman."

The theater doors opened, and Bree appeared with Chase in tow.

"Ah, here we are!" said Mr. O'Malley, all business again. "Son, you must have forgotten about baseball today! I received a call from your coach."

The flush in Chase's cheeks and the frown lines in his forehead made it very clear that he hadn't forgotten, but Chase simply nodded.

"Must have, sir," he said.

"Well, grab your things and let's go," said Mr. O'Malley. "We should make it there right after the seventh-inning stretch!"

Chase's shoulders slouched, but he held up the bag in his hand. "Ready, sir," he said.

"Always thinking ahead. That's my boy!" Mr. O'Malley clapped him on the shoulder. Then he turned to me and Bree. "Ladies, do you need a ride home?"

"No, thank you," said Bree.

Chase's eyes darted to mine.

"I could use a ride," I said. "If you don't mind."

"Not at all!" Mr. O'Malley gestured for us to follow him down the hall, his high spirits returned.

We reached the car, and Chase sat up front with his dad while I climbed in back.

"So, Sunny, did Chase tell you about the no-hitter he pitched in his last game?" asked his dad.

"No, sir," I said. Then, looking over the seat at Chase, I added, "Very nice!"

Chase's gloomy expression lightened a bit. "It was no big deal."

"Are you kidding me?" exclaimed Mr. O'Malley. "Sunny, I'm telling you: My boy's got talent!"

Now Chase was full-on grinning.

"Thanks, Dad," he said.

I wanted to remind him that Chase also had *theater* talent, but I knew my words alone wouldn't matter.

Chase's dad would have to see for himself.

THIRTEEN

EVERY DAY, MY LIST OF tasks was getting longer. When I'd first decided to do my show, all I needed was a script. Now, I not only had to fix Suresh's singing, but also prep for Friday's critiqued performance *and* take care of blocking, costumes, makeup, and scenery.

And if I wanted something done right, I had to do it myself.

Even though there was so little of me to spread around, I was determined to make *Wicked* stand up to *Mary Pops In*. The last thing I needed was for the agent to love Ilana's show more than mine.

Tuesday morning I marched into the cafeteria and approached Cam, the guy playing Mr. Banks, with an offer he couldn't refuse.

"Here's twenty dollars," I said, dropping some wrinkled bills on the table.

He glanced up, startled. "Did I miss something?"

"Sorry. Hi." I smiled at him. "I need a job done, and I need it kept quiet. You in?"

Cam picked up one of the bills. "That depends, 1920s Gangster," he said. "Who do I have to bump off?"

"Ha-ha. It's not *that* kind of job." I dropped into a chair and said in a low voice, "I need you to record two songs for my show. By Thursday."

Cam lowered his voice to match mine. "Don't you have an entire cast for that?"

I shook my head. "One of our lead guys can't sing."

"You mean Suresh?" Cam asked, eating a bite of cereal.

"Shhh!" I glanced around nervously. "And yes. How did you know?"

"He tortures songs during PE," said Cam. "No matter how many dodgeballs we throw at him."

I smoothed out the money I'd tossed on the table. "Could you please do it? I'll even give you credit in the playbill."

Cam chewed his cereal thoughtfully. "Is Suresh okay

with this? I don't want to hurt his feelings."

"Trust me," I said. "His feelings will be hurt way more if people jam pencils in their ears during the show."

Cam laughed. "All right. Give me the lyrics and the music, and I'll get it done." He held out his hand and I placed the money in it.

"By Thursday," I said.

"By Thursday," he promised.

With that chore out of the way, I could focus on my next big dilemma: getting everyone else to sing loud, good, and in harmony. The day before, I thought we'd made tremendous progress from the start of rehearsal to the end. On, Tuesday, however, it felt like we'd taken two huge steps backward.

When I first walked into the theater, everyone was sitting around talking instead of prepping. Then the opening song, which was supposed to be joyful and upbeat, sounded sarcastic and catty.

"Good news," they all sang. "She's *dead*."

I stopped them. "Guys, the Wicked Witch is dead. We should be happy!"

"I failed my math quiz!" Max mourned in a booming voice. "I can't be happy."

"And *Mary Pops In* got a chimney sweep from the

original film to teach them dance moves," said Wendy. "We'll look like fools compared to them!"

Other people chimed in with complaints, and our practice quickly started to collapse.

"Guys," I shouted above them all, "we have to focus. Now, come on. Happy!" I pulled my lips into a smile with my fingers and looked from person to person.

They all attempted to imitate me, but the end result was a lot of sneers and half smiles.

"Uh . . . okay, good enough," I said. "Let's take it from the top."

But instead of singing, they all looked past me into the audience. I turned and almost fell off the stage in surprise.

Grandma was tottering down the aisle toward us.

She waved when she saw me. "Hello, Sunny!"

"Hey, Grandma!" I jumped off the stage and hurried over to her. In a quieter voice, I added, "What are you doing here?"

She rested her purse on a chair.

"I wonder how your show is going," she said, "but I can't ask your parents, so I find out myself." She leaned past me to wave at the others. "Hello!"

They all mumbled hellos, except for Holly, who clapped her palms together and bowed at the waist.

Grandma glanced at me. "What is that?"

"Holly," I said, as if it was enough explanation. I pointed to the chair beside Grandma's purse. "Have a seat. We're working on our opening song."

"Oh, good!" She rubbed her hands together.

I clambered back onstage and whispered, "Guys, that is my grandma. She is our audience. If you can't be happy for me, be happy for her."

I started the music again and, to everyone's credit, they tried, but the song was still lackluster. When it ended, everyone slumped as if it had taken all their energy.

I chanced a peek at Grandma and did a double take. She was now standing on the roof of the orchestra pit and leaning against the stage.

"I didn't feel the song," she said, looking up at me.

"Yeah, we didn't bring it," I said with an apologetic smile. I turned back to the others. "Let's move on to—"

"Again," said Grandma.

I took a steadying breath and counted to three. "Sorry, Grandma?" I asked with a bright smile.

"Do it again," she said, shaking a finger at me. "You can't practice badly once and move on!"

"We didn't practice badly once," Suresh spoke up. "We practiced badly *twice*."

Grandma shook her head. "Then you try again."

The group muttered and moaned.

"Nobody's in the mood, Grandma," I said.

She narrowed her eyes at all of us. "Then you *get* in the mood."

Before I could stop her, she'd hoisted her upper body onto the stage and lifted her right leg, attempting to swing the rest of her body over the edge.

"Grandma, there're stairs," I said as she struggled to bring her left leg up to join the right. "They're probably quicker . . ." Her skirt rode up a few inches. "And less embarrassing for your grandchild."

Derek rushed forward. "Let me help you, ma'am."

He bent to take Grandma's arm, and Cole ran up to grab the other. It was the most awkward stage entrance I'd ever seen, but Grandma didn't seem to notice.

The guys hauled her to her feet, and she thanked them, brushing off her clothes.

"Now," she said, looking at me, "you do not understand the importance of emotion in song."

I nodded. "I do. I told them they need to act happy when they sing a happy song."

Grandma shook her head. "Music is different than theater." She paced in front of us. "Theater is about being someone you are not, acting in a way you do not. Music reveals the truth!"

Several kids murmured in understanding.

"You are not feeling the music," Grandma told us, pounding her fist in her palm for emphasis. "Except you!" she pointed at Holly. "You are happy. I can see that. I can *hear* that."

"Thank you, your . . . your agedness." Holly placed her palms together and bowed.

Grandma just stared at her. "Please get up."

"As you wish," said Holly, bowing again.

I nudged her. "Cool it."

"Sorry." She bowed toward me.

"Holly!"

"It's hard to stop!" she said. I grabbed her by the midsection and straightened her out.

Grandma returned to her pacing. "You need to feel the emotions of the song so the audience *feels* that emotion. Think of something that makes you happy, and *be* happy." She stomped one foot, threw her arms open and a huge smile flashed across her face. "Good neeeeews!" she chirped.

A couple people giggled and others clapped.

"You see?" said Grandma, straightening back up. "You

laugh because you feel my happiness. Because *I* feel it."

"But what if we're not happy?" asked Janice.

"I failed my math quiz!" Max reminded us.

"Yeah, and one of my kittens is sick," said Tim.

That made everyone forget their problems. We all glanced at Tim in surprise.

"*You* ha-have kittens?" asked Cole.

"Yes," said Tim.

"Live ones?" asked Wendy.

Tim frowned. "Yes. How could Fig Mewton be sick if he wasn't alive?"

A couple of the guys snickered.

"You named your kitten Fig Mewton?" asked Suresh.

Tim sighed. "Yes! Because he has a tan body and a brown stomach."

"Awww!" said the girls.

"Can you bring him to practice?" asked Bree.

"Guys!" I lifted my hands above my head but Grandma pulled them down.

"Cat Boy," she said to Tim. "What are the names of your other kittens?"

"Well, I have two," he said. "Kitty Pryde . . ." He got nothing but confused stares, so he explained, "I named her after the girl in *X-Men* who can run through walls."

"You have a cat that can run through walls?" I asked.

"No, but she tries," he said.

Everyone laughed.

"And the other one?" asked Grandma.

"Lotto," said Tim. "Because he likes to be scratched."

Groans and more laughter.

When everyone had calmed down, Grandma had them face the front in a long chorus line. I stood with her off to the side.

"Now," she said, "try the first lines of your song again. Instead of saying 'Good news!' say 'Good *mews*!'"

Everyone laughed harder, and when the music started up, people were still smiling as they belted, "Good meeeeews!"

And it truly sounded as if they had good mews . . . *news* . . . to share.

I hooted and clapped for the others, and Grandma leaned close to me.

"*That* is how you bring happiness to unhappy people," she said.

I nodded. "What was *your* happy thought?"

Grandma put an arm around me. "My granddaughter, of course."

She stayed for the rest of practice, and just her presence

had a profound impact on the cast. They went through the emotions of every song and kept working to get each one right.

When practice ended, Grandma gave me a ride home, and we talked about the show all the way.

"Thanks for your help," I told her. "It really made a difference."

"You are more than welcome." Grandma patted my leg. "Most of you are good singers," she said, "except the Indian boy."

"Yeah, I'm having someone else record his songs," I said. "Luckily, he doesn't mind."

I'd told Suresh the plan at the end of practice. He'd been a little embarrassed but knew it was best for the show . . . and his acting career. I guess enough dodgeballs had finally knocked some sense into him.

"Do you think we'll be able to impress Ms. Elliott this Friday?" I asked.

Grandma looked over at me. "What's this Friday?"

I told her about the ultimatum we'd been given, and Grandma drummed her fingers thoughtfully on the steering wheel.

"The songs will be good," she said. "But to *really* impress, you need a dance number."

"What?!" I cried, causing Grandma to swerve the car. "We have three days! There's no way we can learn a dance number in three days."

"Not a long dance," said Grandma, holding up a finger. "A couple minutes. To add pizzazz."

"Pizzazz?" I stared out the window thoughtfully. "There's an instrumental section in 'Dancing Through Life,'" I said.

"Perfect!" said Grandma. "You could do a waltz."

"I don't know how," I said, working through options in my brain. "But I'll bet I know someone who does."

I took out my phone and pulled up Stefan's number. When he answered, I heard classical music playing in the background.

"Stefan?" I asked. "Did you teach the parrot to play a violin?"

"No," he whispered. "I'm at *Pride and Prejudice* rehearsals, waiting for my next part. What's up?"

"This is going to sound weird, but . . . can you waltz?" I asked.

"I'm a counselor at the STARS program," he scoffed. "Of course I can waltz."

I flashed a thumbs-up at Grandma.

"Next question," I told Stefan. "Can you teach the kids in my show to waltz?"

"Ohhh, that's a tough one," he said. "I guess I could manage an hour to show you the basic moves. When are you thinking? Next week? The week after?"

I grimaced. "Uh . . . tomorrow?"

Stefan got quiet.

"Pretty pretty please?" I begged. "I can't lose this show. There are so many kids depending on it."

Stefan *growled* at me. "Sunny."

"I'll owe you *so* big," I said. "I'll buy fifty tickets to your show!"

"They're ten bucks apiece," he said.

I swallowed hard. "I'll buy *one* ticket to your show!"

Stefan sighed deeply. "Since it's for *you*, I'll come by tomorrow at lunch," he said. "And everyone better be on time and ready to learn."

"Yes! Yes!" I bounced in my seat, feeling a bit like Holly. "Thank you!"

"Gotta go," he said. "My part's coming up."

We hung up, and I beamed at Grandma.

"Problem solved," I said.

She smiled back, but there was a worried look in her eyes. "Good. Now handle *that* one."

She stopped at the entrance to our neighborhood and pointed at the big oak tree.

Chase was sitting beneath it with his arms wrapped around his legs, head hanging as low as it would go.

"He should be at rehearsal," I said, frowning.

I hugged Grandma and jumped out of the car. Chase didn't look up as I sprinted toward the tree. Not even when I sat down beside him.

"Chase?" I said softly.

He finally glanced over at me, and his eyes were rimmed with red, like he'd been crying. He didn't speak; he just stared.

I touched his arm. "Did something happen with the show?"

Chase's nostrils flared and his eyes watered, but he still wouldn't say anything. I placed a hand on his shoulder and felt his muscles tense up.

"He promised I could have this year," said Chase. "Before he 'turned me into a man.'" He puffed himself up and swaggered his upper body.

"He *did* promise," I agreed.

"But then," Chase's voice came out in a squeak, "I told him I'd have to skip a ballgame next week, and he freaked out." He clamped his mouth shut and pounded the back of his head against the tree. I heard bits of bark crackle and fall.

"I'm sorry" was all I could think to say.

He pounded against the tree again, harder this time, and my hands flew up to protect his head.

"Stop! A concussion won't help," I said.

"It might not hurt either." He clenched his teeth and threw his head back.

Of course, this time, my fingers were in the way.

"Ow!" I shrieked as he crushed them against the tree. "It *does* hurt, dummy!" I pushed him forward and clutched my hand to me.

Instantly, the old Chase was back. "Sorry! Are you okay?" He gingerly took my hand and drew it forward where we could both inspect it.

There were a few light scratches and puncture marks but no blood.

"You're lucky," I told him. "You almost broke my autographing hand. Thousands of adoring fans would have been devastated."

He smiled ruefully. "At least *you* still have a chance at adoring fans."

"So do you," I said, flexing my fingers. "People like baseball a *lot* . . . for some reason."

"You'd know if you ever watched one of my games," he said.

"I'll be at the next one," I promised. "Sitting right at midcourt."

"That's basketball," he said.

"Midfield."

"Football," he said.

"Center ice?" I suggested.

We smiled at each other, and I leaned forward to hug him. When I pulled away, his arms held me an extra second so that our faces were inches apart. Chase's eyes studied mine, and I suddenly felt self-conscious.

"I'm sorry about *Mary Pops In*," I said, scooting back a few feet. "I wish your dad could see how much work goes into theater," I said. "Maybe if we asked Ms. Elliott . . ."

Chase wiped the moisture from his eyes. "It won't matter. My dad's never going to change."

He got to his feet and held out a hand to help me up. I wanted to say more but nothing came to mind. I always figured I'd have it made once my name was at the top of the casting sheet.

But I was starting to realize that not even the Chosen Ones had it easy.

FOURTEEN

A COUPLE MINUTES BEFORE NOON THE next day, the Melodramatics were gathered in Blakely Auditorium. I'd told them earlier what I was aiming for, and they came dressed to dance . . . among other things.

"*What* are you wearing?" I asked Suresh.

He bounded onstage in tights and a shirt with huge, billowy sleeves.

"What do you think?" he asked, striking a pose. "These are my dance clothes."

"You look like you're going for Olympic gold in men's figure skating," said Derek.

Suresh glared at him. "At least I'm dressed appropriately."

Derek glanced down at his own outfit, cuffed jeans and a flannel shirt. "What's wrong with this?"

"Nothing. I'm sure you'll make the other lumberjacks proud," said Suresh. "Enjoy the chafing that comes with those pants."

I laughed and Derek glanced at me.

"What about *you*? Are you here to dance or jog on the beach?" asked Derek.

I was wearing a one-piece bathing suit under a pair of shorts. "I haven't danced in a while, okay?" I wrapped my arms around myself. "It doesn't matter anyway. We're all going to look stupid next to—"

The theater doors opened, and Stefan marched in. He pushed sunglasses into his spiky hair and straightened the pinstripe vest he'd worn over a plain white T-shirt. His pants had the same pinstripe but were cuffed at the ankle to reveal sharp black lace-ups.

"Everyone onstage!" he called.

"You're right," said Derek, looking from Stefan's outfit to ours. "We do look stupid."

At Stefan's entry, everyone had paused, but as he leapt deftly onto the stage, we all scrambled to follow his command.

He surveyed all of us, stopping occasionally to study a particular outfit and raise his eyebrows. Then he started counting us off into pairs, except for Anne Marie and Bree, whose characters wouldn't be dancing.

Since I'd be with Suresh, Stefan paired me off with him and placed us toward the front of the stage. The others he arranged at equal distances around us. When he was satisfied, he took a piece of chalk out of his vest pocket and drew squares around our feet on the stage floor.

"Every couple has a square," he said. "The waltz is done in a box step."

He pointed at Bree and gestured her over.

"I need a dance partner," he said.

Bree hurried forward, looking thrilled.

"Gentlemen," said Stefan, "your left arm goes up to shoulder height. Ladies, your right arm goes up to shoulder height. Aaand, join those hands," he said.

It took a few moments since some couples were hesitant.

"I'm not asking you to marry the person you're dancing with," said Stefan. "And I'm fairly certain none of you have cooties. Hold hands, please!"

They all begrudgingly did so.

"Now, gentlemen, your right hand holds your partner

slightly above her waist. Ladies, your *left* hand goes to your partner's shoulder."

There was a lot of mumbling and switching around of hands. At one point, Janice had both hands on Max's shoulders while his were around her waist.

"No, no, no," said Stefan, repositioning their arms. "You aren't trying to lift her into the air. This isn't *Wicked on Ice*."

"If it was, Suresh would be better dressed for it," said Derek.

I had to tighten my grip to keep Suresh from going after him.

Once everyone was in proper form, Stefan moved over to join Bree.

"All right, let's go into the waltz step," Stefan said. "Just watch me and Bree do the first three beats."

After demonstrating with Bree, Stefan gestured to the rest of us. "Let's see what you can do."

That was easier said than done. Stefan snapped the beat, and Suresh moved toward me with his left leg at the same time I moved toward him with my right. Our knees knocked together hard.

"Ow! Sunny, *I'm* the guy! *I* lead!" he said, rubbing his knee.

"Sorry!" I said. "Your shirt distracted me."

Derek wasn't doing any better with Wendy, who kept diving to the side with their joined hands.

"Stop dipping!" he said. "I'm getting seasick!"

The only couple who seemed to be doing well were Cole and Holly, who were dancing in precise, tight squares. I had to give Stefan credit for his infinite patience as he walked from couple to couple, pointing out mistakes. Especially when Suresh smacked him in the face with a billowy sleeve.

"You're not wearing that for the actual performance, are you?" asked Stefan, batting the sleeve away.

"Sunny's in charge of costumes," said Suresh. "Ask her."

I gave Stefan a nervous smile. Truthfully, I hadn't given a thought to what everyone would wear yet.

Well . . . that wasn't entirely true. I'd given plenty of thought to what *I* was going to wear.

"I'm working on it," I said.

"I'd order soon," said Stefan. "It'll take a few weeks for everything to come in, and if it doesn't fit right, you'll have to have it tailored."

"Of course," I said with a nod. Inside, though, my stomach clenched.

Tailoring? Ms. Elliott had said we had a limited budget, and I was pretty sure it didn't include custom fitting for fifteen people.

Stefan moved on to the second three beats, which were a little easier to pick up, and soon we were doing all six beats together.

"One-two-three, one-two-three," he said, moving among the couples and watching us dance. "Girl with the wild arms, your partner looks like he's in pain. Ease up on the movements."

"It's not her dancing," said Derek with a wince. "It's my jeans chafing."

Suresh smirked. "Told you."

Stefan had us dance in our squares for ten minutes before he decided we were ready to go outside our boxes.

"It's time to start moving your partners around the dance floor," he said, taking Bree's arm.

He demonstrated with Bree again, and I had to admit, it looked pretty elegant as they swooped across the stage.

"Your turn," he said to all of us.

Chaos ensued.

Some of the guys were taking gigantic steps and dragging their partners with them. Those who were sticking to small changes soon found themselves being overtaken by the more aggressive dancers.

"Hey, back off!" Suresh yelled at Max and Janice who nearly collided with us.

"Move faster!" shouted Max.

"It's a *timed* beat," said Suresh. "If we move faster, it's not a waltz, it's jogging."

Nevertheless, Suresh took a bigger step and almost knocked Derek and Wendy off the stage.

"Dude!" said Derek with a scowl. "I know those huge sleeves let you fly, but some of us can't!"

"Sorry," I said. "We're trying to avoid the other dancers." I nodded to Max and Janice, who were fast approaching.

Derek's face relaxed. "It's cool. Just . . . be careful."

"Watch your spacing!" Stefan shouted. "If you're close enough to spit on another couple, you're too close."

"Janice is close enough to spit on someone across the room!" one of the other girls said snidely.

"Shut up, Stacey!" said Janice, sprinkling Max on the face.

"Guys," I warned. "We don't need Ms. Elliott to know we can't even *dance* without fighting. Focus on your footwork."

Everyone quieted down, and Stefan made the bold

move to add the music we'd be dancing to in the scene. People started to stumble a bit, but he snapped his fingers to get them back on track.

"Now," he said. "Look at the dancers around you."

We did. And we smiled.

"You guys look awesome," said Anne Marie from the sideline.

I had to agree.

At the end of the hour, everyone thanked Stefan and dashed off to eat lunch before next class. Except me. I hung back to ask him a favor.

"Another one?" he asked, jumping down from the stage. "You realize even genies only grant so many wishes."

"Yes, but I can pay this time!" I said. I fished through my backpack and pulled out an envelope. "Here. Two hundred dollars."

I'd cleared out almost all of my personal savings for this favor. The only thing left in my bank was three quarters and some lint.

Stefan sighed and crossed his arms. "Before I take anything, let me decide if I can even *grant* this favor."

"It's about Chase," I said. "His dad pulled him from *Mary Pops In* because he thinks theater is silly and pointless."

I could almost see the spikes in Stefan's hair stand on end. "I see," he said in an even voice.

"So I was hoping you'd help me show him the power a little performing can have."

One corner of Stefan's mouth curled up in a smile. "Go on."

I told him my plan, and the more I explained, the broader his smile got.

"What do you think?" I asked when I was finished.

Stefan scratched his chin. "Just so you know, what you're asking will take a couple weeks. It won't be done in time to get him back into *Mary Pops In*," he said.

I shook my head. "It doesn't matter. This isn't about one moment in his life. This is about his entire future."

Stefan threw an arm around me and pulled me close for a hug. "That is the most mature thing I've ever heard you say. All right, I'm in."

"For free?" I asked hopefully.

"Uh . . . no," said Stefan, sliding the envelope out of my hand. "In fact, I should be charging you way more."

He had a point. My plan required eight people besides Chase.

"Okay," I agreed and hugged him back. "Thank you so much for everything," I said.

"Good luck with Ms. Elliott," he told me. "And come by the shop Friday to let me know how it goes."

I nodded and watched him leave, hoping what he'd taught us would be enough.

Cam was better than his word, getting me the disc of recorded songs the very next morning.

"Oooh, thank you so much!" I told him.

"No problem," he said. "And good luck. I hope you guys sell a lot of tickets for your show."

I looked up from slipping the disc in my backpack. "What do you mean?" I asked with a confused smile. "We're part of the same showcase as you."

Cam shook his head. "Our shows are the same night, but we're charging admission separately to help with the budget crunch. It was Ilana's idea."

Of course it was. Anything to separate her show from the "freak show."

"Well, thanks, and good luck to you guys, too," I said.

Cam leaned in and talked out of the corner of his mouth. "And if you . . . uh . . . need any more favors," he said in his best gangster accent, "you know where to find me, dollface."

I rolled my eyes and grinned. "Good-bye, Cam."

He winked and strolled away.

Later that day I ran into Bree and Suresh and gave him the disc. I didn't bother mentioning the separate ticket sales; that would only bum them out.

"Make sure you listen to Cam's voice and practice," I told Suresh. "So you can move your mouth at the exact same time his voice comes out."

"Yeah, yeah, I know," said Suresh, flipping the disc over and over in his hands.

Bree rubbed his arm. "Don't be sad. You can't be good at *everything*."

Suresh scowled at her. "Who says I'm good at *anything*?"

"You're good at doing splits," I said. "And you're a good dancer."

"And a *great* boyfriend," said Bree, gazing up at him admiringly.

Suresh grinned sheepishly. "All these things are true."

"So just practice hard," I said. "Both of you. Remember . . . there's an agent in the audience."

That became my motivational chant to the Melodramatics any time I saw one of them.

"To get into character, let's come up with a playlist of our character's favorite songs. And practice hard. There's an agent in the audience!"

On Thursday, it became, "Let's step into our characters

for the entire day, even during school. And practice hard. There's an agent in the audience!"

Friday at lunch, when I gathered everyone for a final run-through, the first thing Suresh said was, "Sunny, please no more character exercises. The voices in my head are keeping me up at night."

"Yeah, and people were *really* annoyed when I followed them around and narrated their lives," said Tim.

I smiled. "Sorry, guys. But don't forget—"

"There's an agent in the audience!" several people shouted.

We all laughed, and I held up my hands.

"Okay, okay. You get the point!"

In our brief rehearsal we maneuvered through dance steps and the trickier songs. I had to give Suresh credit. He was mouthing the lyrics so precisely, it was almost impossible to tell the voice coming over the speakers wasn't his. I was pretty pleased with our progress, and I really hoped Ms. Elliott would notice.

When she walked into Blakely Auditorium that afternoon, the Melodramatics were lined up onstage, scripts clutched behind their backs.

"Good afternoon, everyone," said Ms. Elliott, settling into the front row with a clipboard.

"Good afternoon," we all chorused.

She smiled at us. "I understand you've been working on a show, and I'd like to see it."

I cleared my throat. "We'd like to share it with you."

Ms. Elliott held her arms open. "Please."

The Melodramatics scrambled offstage or into position. I nodded at Cole to cue the music, and the show began.

And quickly fell apart.

It was definitely a two-week-old performance. Some of the lines were nervously rushed, and there were awkward pauses where kids missed their cues. I hated to admit it, but we were nowhere near as good as the *Mary Pops In* cast.

But—Ms. Elliott sat through the entire show and didn't yell at us once for ruining the good name of theater. Occasionally, she'd jot something on her clipboard when we were speaking, and during the songs, she tapped her foot.

And for our dance number? She smiled and leaned back in her chair.

Score one for Grandma.

An hour and a half after Ms. Elliott held out her arms for the show to begin, she was drawing them toward her to applaud our finale.

I motioned to the other Melodramatics, and we gathered at the edge of the stage to hear her judgment.

"For a production run by students who"—she paused—"to be honest, haven't acted much, I'm impressed. Although, I did have some critiques to improve your performance for opening night."

I grabbed the hands of the people on either side of me. "Opening night?" I repeated. "So we get to keep our show?"

Ms. Elliott pushed her glasses into place and studied all of us. "Of course," she said.

An explosion of cheers and squeals followed, and it took several minutes and a booming "Quiet!" from Max to restore silence. We listened earnestly to Ms. Elliott's critiques, and when she was done, I excused the rest of the cast to have a private word with her.

"Thank you so much for giving us a chance," I said as she handed me the notes from her clipboard. "Once we get the costumes and makeup and scenery taken care of, it'll look even better," I promised.

"It looks wonderful now," she assured me with a quick smile. Then she placed a hand on my shoulder. "But while we're on the subject, I wanted to discuss your budget."

I glanced down at the hand she'd placed on me and felt a huge weight come with it.

"Yes?" I dared to ask.

"I'm afraid," she said, "that I have bad news."

FIFTEEN

THERE ARE TWO KINDS OF bad news.

1. Expected: "Sunny, I'm cutting you off from coffee because it's affecting the show. There was no Daddy Starbucks in *Annie*."

2. Unexpected: "Sunny, we're still having budget issues with *Mary Pops In*. I have to take most of your funding."

That was the bombshell Ms. Elliott chose to drop on me. My mouth fell open and all I could make was a croaking sound.

"I'm truly sorry," she continued. "But after we resolved the disaster with prop expenses, we still had to consider the *tailoring*." She held a weary hand to her forehead.

"Do you really need fitted costumes?" I ventured. "Kids grow every day. By the time the show opens, everyone could be busting seams like the Incredible Hulk."

Ms. Elliott frowned. "I wish we *could* do without tailoring, but Ilana made a good point. We'll have STARS members in the audience, and we can't afford to look sloppy."

Who cared what the STARS members thought? *I* was going to have an agent in the audience! I bit the inside of my cheek to keep from screaming.

"What about the kids in my show?" I asked. "You don't want *us* to look sloppy, do you?"

"Well, that's the good thing, dear," Ms. Elliott said, squeezing my shoulder. "With the money left in your budget, you *could* get tailoring done to . . . whatever you find in the wardrobe room." She gestured vaguely behind the stage.

I'd seen the outfits in the wardrobe room. They were from previous shows, had been sweated in multiple nights, and needed more disinfecting than *any* budget could afford.

"What about special effects?" I asked.

"You can use the greatest special effect of all," said Ms. Elliott with a whimsical smile. She pointed to her head. "Your imagination!"

I stared at her. "My imagination won't keep me airborne

if I jump from the stage rafters," I said. "Trust me. I tried something similar in a cape."

Ms. Elliott sighed and took my hands. "I'm sorry, Sunny, but this is the way things are. And frankly, you're lucky to be doing a show at all."

Her words sounded dangerously close to a threat. In fact, they sounded more like . . .

"You're not letting us keep our show because we *deserve* it," I said. "You're doing it because you feel bad taking away everything else."

Ms. Elliott released my hands. "Don't be ridiculous. I think it was an apt performance."

"Apt" sounded one step above "I didn't hate it," but I knew better than to push it further.

"Okay, then," I said. "What's my new budget?"

Ms. Elliott only hesitated a second before saying, "A thousand dollars."

My heart sank into my stomach. "A thousand dollars?! That *barely* covers props!"

Ms. Elliott had reached her sympathy quota for the day. "I know you'll make it work," she said, patting my arm. "You're a clever girl."

I didn't respond. Instead, I snatched my bag out of a chair and stormed out the emergency exit, letting the screaming alarms match the screaming in my head.

I tried and I tried, but no matter what I did, something fought me at every turn, trying to pull me down. It was getting harder and harder to stand back up. Maybe the universe wanted me to just give up.

Maybe the universe thought I sucked.

After all, the only way I could get into a show was to create one of my own. How pathetic was that? I mean, sure, Ilana had played a big part in my exclusion, but what about all the shows before this one? I obviously wasn't included for a reason.

Tears welled in my eyes, blurring the street signs. I wiped at the dampness and hurried to catch the crosstown bus. My phone buzzed in my pocket, but I ignored it. The only person I felt like talking to now was Stefan.

When I appeared in the shop door, he glanced up in surprise, then concern, as I burst into tears. I tried to blubber an explanation but it was difficult to do while crying *and* running toward him.

"Oh, Sunny. Did Ms. Elliott cancel the show?" he asked, leaning over to hug me.

I shook my head into his shirt. "The show's . . . still . . . on," I managed.

Stefan stepped back. "So these are violent, *happy* tears?"

I shook my head again and took a deep breath. "Ms. Elliott cut our budget to almost nothing, and she's letting us keep the show as an act of pity."

The bell above the door rang, but Stefan didn't even look up.

"How much is almost nothing?" he asked.

"Our costumes will probably be made from cafeteria napkins," I said, sniffling.

Stefan grimaced. "You're talking a thousand dollars, huh?"

"Yes," I said. "This show is doomed. Everything and everyone is against us."

The bells over the door rang again, and this time he left to greet the customer. He returned with a box of tissues and a wriggling puppy.

"I trust you know which is for petting, and which is for blowing your nose," he said, holding out both.

I smiled gratefully and took just the puppy, which squirmed until it could lean back and lick my nose.

"So the odds are stacked against you," said Stefan, "but you've prevailed so far."

"It's not just money." I hugged the puppy close. "It's our singing. And our acting. And our dancing."

Stefan frowned. "As your one-hour dance instructor, I'm mildly offended."

"Okay," I said. "The dancing's not horrible, but the rest of the show stinks. If it was just me, that'd be an easy fix. But *everyone* is just as bad, if not worse."

Stefan pursed his lips. "Is this the wrong time to say 'I told you so'?"

I scowled and thrust the puppy in his face. "Don't make me use this."

"I'm *kidding*," he said. "You're being too hard on yourself and everyone else. You didn't really think you'd be ready for Broadway right off the bat, did you?"

He motioned for me to follow him down a line of fish tanks.

"I don't know . . . maybe," I said. "At least I thought mentioning the agent in the audience would motivate everyone."

Stefan stopped and looked at me. "The agent that's coming to see you?" he asked.

I blushed. "I may have left that part out. My point is . . . we're nowhere near as perfect as the kids in *Mary Pops In*."

"Perfect?" Stefan grunted in amusement. "No offense,

Sunny, but no one at your school is perfect. *I'm* not even perfect."

I actually smiled. "You mean The Great Stefan has flaws?"

"Yes," he muttered out of the corner of his mouth, "but don't spread that around."

"Okay, fine, so we're far from the best," I said. "But we're also far from *Mary Pops In* quality."

Stefan fished around in his apron and pulled out a dog biscuit, which was quickly snatched away by the puppy.

"That's not a fair comparison," he said. "Don't forget that most of the kids in your show have never spoken more than a couple lines. They have way more learning to do."

I considered this for a moment while he took a lid off one of the fish tanks.

"Even if that's true," I said, "how do we avoid looking stupid with our budget?"

Stefan shrugged and sprinkled food into one of the tanks. "You're not starting from scratch. CAA has old props and costumes that'll work if you just use—"

"Don't say 'our imaginations,'" I said. "Or I will shove your head in the piranha tank."

"I was going to say 'supplies from the art department,'" said Stefan, giving me a look.

"Oh. Sorry," I said.

When he finished feeding the fish, I handed him back the puppy. "Thanks for the loaner. And for listening."

"Are you gonna be okay now?" he asked, giving me another hug.

I nodded. "I should probably go let everyone know what happened with the show. *And* let you get back to your customers." I pointed to a group of kids browsing the cat toys.

They turned to look at us, and I realized with horror that I recognized them all . . . my shouter, my spitter, and my creepy-eyed narrator.

Max, Janice, and Tim had been standing one aisle over the whole time.

And they'd heard every word I said.

There was no doing damage control with this one. Not after three people heard me bash them and the show firsthand. I chanced a look at Stefan, but even he looked unsure of what to do.

Finally, he said, "Hey, I heard Ms. Elliott approved your show! Let me get you each a congratulatory goldfish."

Then he abandoned me to fend for myself.

It was fitting that I was in a store called Feathers 'N' Fangs, because the three kids now staring at me looked ready to bare their teeth and go for my throat.

"Guys," I said. "Let me explain."

"Too late," said Janice, holding up her cell phone. Max and Tim followed suit. "Everyone in the play now knows how pathetic you think we are."

I held up a finger. "I never said pathetic."

"No." Max's voice made the birds screech in their cages. "But you said the show stank and that everyone is just as bad as, if not worse than, you."

"Not to mention, you lied to us about the agent," added Janice.

I blushed. "Okay, I did do that."

"We've been talking about it the last few days . . . all of us," said Tim.

Suddenly, those prerehearsal gatherings I walked in on made more sense.

"And we're acting on everyone's behalf," said Max, "to tell you that you're through."

I crossed my arms over my chest. "What's that supposed to mean?"

"It means that you're out of the show," said Max.

"What?!" My eyes grew even bigger than Tim's. "You can't do that! It's *my* show."

"It *was* your show," said Janice, her spit sailing farther

than usual. "But you obviously don't care about it *or* us, so we're saving it from you."

"No." I shook my head. "You're wrong, I *do* care. I know I had my doubts, but we can make it work."

There was no way Bree would let this happen. I pulled my phone out of my pocket and dialed her, but there was no answer. I tried Suresh with the same result.

"Why don't you ask the *Mary Pops In* cast for your part back?" asked Max. "Then you can be in a *good* show."

"I didn't mean what I said." I looked from him to Tim to Janice. "I was just upset. I love this show too much to watch it fail." Tears pricked at my eyes, and Janice's started watering too.

"We looked up to you," she said.

"And you still can," I promised. "I'll take care of our budget problem. That'll show how much I believe in us!"

"I wouldn't count on it!" Max shouted after me.

But I was already out the door, calling Chase.

"Hey, Sunny! What's up?" he answered the phone.

I glanced over my shoulder nervously.

"I may have done a terrible, terrible thing," I whispered.

Chase got quiet.

"If I hang up now, how much jail time do I avoid?" he asked.

"It's nothing criminal!" I said, rolling my eyes. "I told Stefan how terrible everyone in my show was and that I'd lied about hooking people up with an agent. And some kids from the show overheard."

Chase whistled through his teeth. "You were better off committing a crime."

"That's why I'm calling the politician's son to help me out of this mess," I said. "Can you meet me somewhere?"

"How about in a couple hours?" he asked. "I'm still at rehearsal."

"Thanks," I said.

Then a thought occurred to me.

Chase was at *rehearsal*.

"Wait," I said. "Are you back in *Mary Pops In*?"

I could hear him grinning through the phone. "Ms. Elliott convinced my dad I had to be in the show as part of my grade. It was Ilana's idea. Awesome, right?"

I'd given away my *entire* savings . . . money I could have put toward the show . . . on a secret plan to get Chase back into acting. And in one fell swoop, Ilana, Queen of the Life Ruiners, had beaten me to it.

I didn't know whether to laugh or cry.

Since I'd already done plenty of the second, I just smiled and said, "That's great, Chase."

"Yeah. Although my dad refuses to go," he said. "Ilana said she'd talk to him for me."

I rolled my eyes again. "If anyone can save the day, it's her," I said.

"She's the best," Chase agreed. "I mean, she has time to worry about me, even with all the stuff going on in *her* life."

I snorted. "What stuff? The play she wormed her way into?"

"Uh . . . no," said Chase in an odd voice. "Her mom got laid off after she broke her arm, remember?"

I lifted the phone from my ear and stared at it in confusion. "Laid off?" I repeated. "Broken arm?"

"Yeah, from the car accident. I thought you knew," said Chase. "She and her mom are strapped for cash."

I stopped in my tracks.

That was why Ilana had been pushing makeovers so hard. That was why she'd taken money from Chase for her notes. And that was probably why she was being so crazy about *Mary Pops In*.

"Sunny?" said Chase. "Oak tree in two hours?"

"Sure," I said. "And congrats on getting the part. Again."

Chase laughed. "Thanks. Bye, Sunny."

Grandma's car was in the driveway when I got home, and I hurried up the steps, trying to think of a secret way I could tell her about the afternoon and Ilana.

As I walked into the living room, I smelled jasmine tea and saw her and Mom sitting on the couch. They glanced up, and I waved.

"Hi, Mom! Hi, Grandma!"

"Hi, Sunny," said Mom, taking a sip of tea. "How was *Wicked* rehearsal?"

SIXTEEN

I STOOD FROZEN TO THE SPOT. My eyes darted to Grandma.

"Don't look to her for help," said Mom, calmly adding cream to her tea. "She's the one who told me."

"Grandma!" I groaned.

Grandma shrugged apologetically. "Her truth kimchi must be stronger than mine."

I turned to Mom. "Okay, no, I'm not in the official school musical, and I'm sorry I didn't tell you the truth. But I had a good reason!"

Mom patted the couch cushion beside her. "Sit, Sunny. Your grandmother already told me."

I sat and waited for whatever punishment came with lying about a show. No auditioning for future ones?

Mom seemed to be reading my mind. "I'm tempted to keep you out of this show for lying to us."

"I'm not in a show anymore," I told her, staring at the carpet.

Grandma made an indignant noise and sat up straight. "Ms. Elliott didn't approve? After all that hard work?"

"She approved it," I said. "I'm just not in it."

For a moment, Mom forgot she was upset. "But it was *your* show."

"Not after I insulted the cast and lied to them about an agent," I said in a quiet voice.

"Sunny!" Mom and Grandma scolded at the same time.

"I know!" I buried my face in my hands. "I messed everything up. With everyone."

Mom sighed and patted my back. "You didn't mess everything up. It just hurts me that you felt you needed to hide the truth."

I peeked through my fingers at her. "I'm sorry."

"Would we have been happy if you got a lead role in *Mary Pops In*?" Mom continued. "Absolutely. Would we have been devastated if you didn't? Of course not."

"*You* wouldn't have been upset," I scoffed. "*You*. My

actress mother. Who's trying to get me an agent."

"There will always be other shows, Sunny," said Mom with a casual wave of her hand. "If you don't get into this one, you get into the next."

"But you were so proud when you thought I was in," I said. "And you seemed a lot happier to have me as your daughter."

"Happier?" Mom clucked her tongue and held open her arms, gesturing me to her. I leaned over and snuggled against her shoulder.

"I was *happier* because it was something we could share," she said, kissing the top of my head. "Every year, you get older and every year we talk less, because your father and I aren't 'cool.'"

"*That's* not true." I twisted around to look up at her. "Why do you think I want to be like you when I grow up?"

Mom smiled and pinched my nose. "I don't want you to be like me," she said. "I want you to be like you. Okay?"

I sat up and hugged her. "Okay."

"As far as punishment," she said, and I winced. "Two weeks of being grounded is fair, don't you agree?"

I perked up. "Only two weeks? Really?" I scooted back and narrowed my eyes. "What's the catch?"

Mom laughed. "No catch. Your show has helped quite a few kids from what your grandmother says."

Grandma leaned forward. "It's true. They all look up to you."

Her words reminded me of Janice's, and I immediately slumped on the couch.

"Yeah, they *did* look up to me," I said. "I was a pretty good director . . . up until the end."

Mom's eyebrows shot up. "You were directing *and* acting?"

She sounded impressed, and I couldn't help grinning.

"A little bit," I said.

"Well, I need more details," said Mom, lifting the teapot to pour me a cup. Only a few drops rolled out. "And we need more tea."

Grandma hoisted herself off the couch. "I'll get it," she said, and I started filling Mom in.

I told her about the crazy auditions and the crazier kids, and she laughed. I told her about all the things we'd been through, individually and as a group, and she hugged me. When I told her about Ilana and the budget crunch, though, she held up a hand and left the room.

"Where's she going?" I asked Grandma, who had rejoined us on the couch.

"I think this is what they call sending for reinforcements," said Grandma.

"No, it's called killing two birds with one stone." Mom reappeared with a phone by her ear. "We're going to get you back into that show *and* take care of your wardrobe problem. How many kids are in your show?" she asked.

I wrinkled my forehead. "Uh . . . fifteen, including me. Why?"

"Fifteen," Mom said into the phone. There was a pause. "*Wicked*. Anything from *Wizard of Oz* should work too." Pause. "Carnegie Arts Academy, Monday afternoon." Mom listened intently and then thanked whoever was on the other line before ending the call.

Grandma and I watched her expectantly.

"On Monday afternoon a van from Disguise the Limit will be at your school," said Mom. "They're a costume company, and they'll be bringing clothes that might fit your show."

My teacup slipped through my fingers, and I barely caught it before it hit my lap. "Are you serious?!" I squealed.

Mom smiled. "Anything to help my daughter."

I put down my teacup and bounced across the room. "Thank you so so so much!" I squeezed Mom around the middle.

"You're welcome," she said with a laugh.

Dad stepped through the doorway and paused to watch us. "What's going on *here*?" he asked with an amused grin.

"I'm helping Sunny get costumes for her show," said Mom.

Dad tilted his head to one side. "I thought the school took care of everything for *Mary Pops In*."

I met Mom's eyes, and we laughed.

"It does," I said. "But I've got a funny story for you, Dad."

On Monday morning, I staggered into school under the weight of a box bearing fourteen gifts. It would've been easier to unload them if all the Melodramatics had been in one place, but I hadn't been able to reach anyone besides Bree all weekend. She, thankfully, had forgiven me, but I still had a ton of apologies to issue.

The first person I spotted was Max, and when he saw me almost drop the box, he instinctively reached out to help.

"Thanks," I said. "And I'm sorry."

Max put the box on the ground and stared at me.

"This whole show was your dream, Sunny," he said with a frown . . . and an oddly quiet voice. "I was really proud of everything we did. But if you can't believe in the show, how can we?"

"You're right," I said, reaching into the box. "You've all worked really hard, which is why *this* is for you."

I held out a small trophy filled with candy and a note card. Max examined the engraving on the trophy.

"Best actress?" he asked in his usual loud voice.

"Whoops!" I blushed and handed him a different one. "Here. Best actor."

Max smiled despite himself. "And what's this?"

He opened the card and read it aloud.

"'I've been wicked and I know it. But I'm sorry; let me show it. Be at Blakely this afternoon for a wardrobe extravaganza.'"

Max raised an eyebrow. "Seriously?"

I shrugged. "I guess you won't find out unless you show up."

He grinned and nodded. "All right. I'll be there."

I smiled and picked up my box to find the next person, my load already a little lighter.

That afternoon, all fourteen Melodramatics met me in the theater with mixed emotions on their faces. Some, like Bree and Max, looked open-minded. Others, like Suresh and Janice, were stony-faced.

I paced in front of them, going over the speech Chase had helped me work out in my mind.

"On Friday," I said, "I did something stupid. I let all the little problems we've been having get to me." I stared at my hands. "And I said some really horrible things."

Nobody spoke.

"Usually, there's a whole support team to handle issues, but since it's just me, it's a little harder." I opened my arms. "We've only been doing this for two weeks. I can't expect us to be brilliant. It takes time and practice."

Several people muttered their agreement.

"But," I held up a finger, "we also have to be *willing* to put in the time and practice. Theater is hard work, and in the real world, some actors are on set fourteen hours a day. I'm just asking for a *couple* hours a day."

"And weekends," someone in the back added.

Beside me, Bree's face darkened, and she glared at the crowd.

"Hey!" she barked. In the front row, Suresh's eyes widened. "It's only for six weeks!"

People gaped at her, awestruck. She cleared her throat and in her usual, quiet voice added, "If you can't handle that, you're in the wrong business."

I grinned. "What she said."

From the center of the crowd, a hand went up to a chorus of "Ow!"

"Yes, Wendy," I said.

"What about the agent?" she asked.

I sighed. "That was a bad way to try and motivate you, and I'm sorry I lied. *But* my mom doesn't see why the agent can't keep an open mind about everyone."

The group buzzed excitedly.

And then there was a different buzzing. From the theater loading dock.

"I think the costumes are here," I said.

People cheered, and I couldn't help asking, "So can you forgive me?"

"Yes!" they chorused.

I smiled. "Then let's see what we've got."

We hustled as a group to the loading dock door, and Derek and Cole lifted it open. A yellow van with Disguise the Limit emblazoned on the side was parked with its back end facing the theater.

"This is so exciting!" chirped Holly. "Like Christmas and my birthday and Columbus Day all at once!"

"You celebrate Columbus Day?" asked Suresh.

The driver of the costume van sauntered over.

"Sunny Kim?" he asked.

"Yes! That's me!" I waved my hand and hurried forward.

He held out a clipboard. "Sign for delivery, please."

I did so, and the driver handed me a copy.

"Where do you want me to leave the racks?" he asked, unfolding a ramp at the back of the van.

"Leave them?" I asked. "We don't choose the outfits right now?"

The driver snorted. "You think I'm waiting around for a theater cast to pick costumes? I've seen how stage divas can get."

I laughed. "We're not divas. If anything—"

"Suspenders were *my* idea! Nobody else can wear them!" Suresh told Max and Cole.

I cleared my throat and smiled at the driver. "Maybe just leave the racks here."

He nodded. "You got it."

I walked over to Suresh and punched him in the arm.

"Ow! You're back in the show for two minutes, and already you're violent?" he asked.

"Quit acting like a diva!" I said. "You can't claim sole ownership of suspenders."

Suresh frowned, rubbing his arm. "But how will people tell us apart?" He glanced at Cole and Max.

Cole and Max glanced at me.

"Should *we* let him know he's Indian, or do you want to?" Max asked.

Just in time, the driver rolled out the first clothing rack, and it was *stuffed* with costumes.

Everyone *ooh*ed and *aah*ed.

"Look at all the dresses!" marveled Bree, sifting through one side.

"Sunny, you *are* forgiven," said Wendy.

The driver arrived with a second rack. "And one for the fellas," he said.

"Nice!" I fished out a shirt and vest. "This'll be perfect for the school scenes."

"Uh . . . Sunny?" Derek walked around the side of the rack, holding a pair of pants. "I know we're supposed to be Munchkins, but . . ." He held the pants up to his waist. The bottom cuffs dragged several feet on the ground.

"Wow," I said. "You *really* need a growth spurt to kick in."

Derek frowned at me.

"I'm kidding," I said. "These look like adult costumes. The driver must—" I turned toward the van, but it was already zooming across the parking lot on its way out.

"Huh." I chewed my lip. "He probably had a costume emergency come up."

"Sure," said Derek. "Someone shrank their ballgown in the dryer." He gave me a withering look.

I patted his arm reassuringly. "We'll figure it out. Let's just get these inside so we can try some on."

A few of the guys wheeled in the racks, and we gathered on stage to see what we had to work with.

"Let's start with the guys," I said.

There was a lot of commotion as shirts and pants were pulled from the rack.

"If you take something and don't want it, put it on the floor!" I shouted.

After about fifteen minutes, there was a huge pile of discarded clothes on the stage, but each guy had at least the top part of his ensemble. The trousers were a different story.

"They're all too long!" said Derek.

"Do you guys have any nice pants of your own you can wear?" I asked.

There were a few nods mixed in with a chorus of no's.

"If you have them, wear them," I said. "The rest of you are going to have to make do with these," I said. "Or take what's in the wardrobe room."

The guys didn't look thrilled by either prospect.

I grabbed the pair of pants Derek had chosen and

studied the hem. "I think I have an idea how to fix this. Be right back. Girls, start choosing your costumes."

I hopped off the stage and ran into the art supply room, stealing one of their heavy-duty staplers. When I came back, the girls were still choosing and the guys were doing their best to help.

"How about this one?" Max held a dress out to Janice.

"For the school scene?" she asked. "No."

When she'd started talking, Max had thrown his arms up to protect his face. But as she spoke, he lowered them, wide-eyed.

"Hey, you didn't spit at all!" he cried.

Janice grinned, revealing straight, white teeth. "I finally got my braces off today. Thanks for noticing."

"Wow," whispered Max. "Nice teeth."

Janice blushed.

Max glanced down at the dress he was holding. "So why not this?"

"For one thing, it's an evening gown," she said.

"But it would look nice on you," he said.

Janice blushed. "I'll save it for the dance number."

I put a hand on Anne Marie's shoulder. "You know what you're looking for, right?"

She nodded and smirked. "Blah blah black."

Wendy, who was playing the headmistress, had already put on a costume and was trying in vain to raise her arms above her head.

"I can barely move," she said.

"Perfect!" someone called.

"Not nice!" I called back. I smiled at Wendy. "But . . . yeah, I think that works."

"Sunny!" Derek was standing by the guy's clothes, holding out the pair of pants.

"Right!" I waved my stapler. "Hold them still."

Bree came forward to watch. "Why don't we use the budget money to get the pants tailored?" she asked.

I shook my head. "We'll probably need it for all kinds of last-minute stuff."

"But—"

"Bree, relax," I said. "I've got everything under control."

I punched in staples all along the bottom of the trousers. While I worked, Anne Marie wandered over.

"All this green reminds me," she said, "I need to have green skin."

I squinted thoughtfully. "I think there should be a makeup kit in the wardrobe room," I said.

Bree made a disgusted face. "Couldn't we just buy some new stuff?"

"From where?" I asked. "Halloween's been over for months. Besides, we need the money for other things."

"Like scenery?" asked Anne Marie, glancing around.

I snapped my fingers. "Exactly! I need to order some scenery. Bree, show Anne Marie where the makeup in the wardrobe room is."

Bree sighed and walked off with Anne Marie in tow.

I put the final staple in Derek's trousers and held them up.

"There!" I said. "Perfect."

"Yeah," said Derek, "as long as I don't go through any metal detectors."

I rolled my eyes. "Go try them on, please?"

Derek hurried offstage and I moved on to see who else I could help. After a few minutes, I heard Bree calling my name.

"Sunny, I think Anne Marie's allergic to the makeup." Bree pulled her onstage. Anne Marie's face was green and swollen to twice its size, her frightened eyes peeking out.

"Augh!" everyone screamed.

"Sunny, I'm not fat enough for these." Derek trotted onstage, holding his pants up by the waist. When he saw Anne Marie, his hands flew up to cover his mouth.

Then his pants fell off.

"Augh!" everyone screamed again.

I sighed. "I am *so* glad this happened after Ms. Elliott's visit."

"And I think I know what we're spending our budget on," said Bree, rubbing Anne Marie's shoulder.

I glanced at her. "A trip to the emergency room?"

She nodded. "I'll get the nurse."

SEVENTEEN

THERE'S NOTHING QUITE LIKE EXPLAINING to an ambulance driver that a girl's green skin is perfectly normal. Or explaining to a crowd of *Mary Pops In* actors that they won't catch "puffy gangrene."

At least I'd made up with the Melodramatics and gotten everyone their costumes, even if they didn't fit properly. And when I saw Ilana watching us from across the theater, I decided it was time to take care of something else.

"We need to talk," I told her.

Ilana crossed her arms. "Why? So you can yell and threaten to hurt me?"

I shook my head. "No yelling. No threats. If I say I'm

going to hurt you, I really will. I promise." I tried for a smile, and after a hesitant moment, Ilana tried too.

"All right," she said, stepping closer. "Where should we go? The control booth?"

I shook my head. "It probably still smells like farts."

Ilana wrinkled her forehead. "Huh?"

"Never mind," I said. "How about the wardrobe room? I need costumes from there anyway."

A guilty look washed over Ilana's face.

"Sure," she said, leading the way.

"Chase told me about your mom," I said as we walked. "Is she okay? Other than the arm, I mean."

Ilana nodded. "The car's a mess, though. The trunk won't open, and we had to tape plastic over one of the back windows." She got quiet. "It's really embarrassing."

I wasn't sure how to respond. The one time my dad had been in a car accident, he'd had the car fixed that week and rented a nice one while he waited.

"That must suck," I finally said, and opened the door to the wardrobe room.

It didn't smell as bad as I'd imagined. Like mothballs and plastic from all the synthetic costumes. I pulled out a pair of colonial-style breeches, and with it came a huge spider.

"*Augh!*" Ilana and I both screamed. I stomped on the spider, but Ilana took the pants and hurled them across the room.

"Hey, I'm gonna need those!" I protested. "We just got our budget cut."

Ilana blushed. "Sorry."

"About throwing the pants?" I asked, retrieving them. "Or telling Ms. Elliott to cut our budget?"

Ilana didn't answer.

"At least tell me this," I said. "Why are you so bent on bringing me down?"

She shook her head. "I'm not. This was never about you. I just really need this show to go perfectly."

"Ugh! You keep—!" I stopped when I realized I was yelling. "Sorry. You keep saying that. Why?"

Ilana sighed. "Because I can't go to the STARS program unless it does."

I wrinkled my forehead in confusion. "You've already been accepted."

Ilana shook her head again. "It's . . . the tuition." She dropped down to the floor. "I don't have the money to get in, but if the STARS people find out, they'll give my spot to someone else."

I sat on the floor beside her. “So why have them in the audience at all?”

“They offer an award,” she said, “to a certain number of kids they think are outstanding in their field . . . acting, directing, music, or dance. And with the award, they give free tuition.”

Now all the pieces were starting to fit together. Ilana needed to be in the best play as the best actress so she could win the STARS award. But *nobody* could know how badly she needed the money or she’d be out of the program.

“Wow,” I said. “*That* is a lot of pressure.”

She snorted. “You’re telling me.”

I gave her a pained look. “But did it have to come at my expense? Or anyone else’s?”

Ilana held out her hands, palms up. “I don’t have another option. *You* can afford coaches and your parents are connected. This is just a school play to you, but it means everything to me.” Ilana stared at her lap.

As twisted as her logic was, I couldn’t be entirely mad at her anymore. I also couldn’t let her keep ruining things for me.

But I *could* let her make my show even better.

“I’ll make you a deal,” I said. “Because clearly, we need

help in the makeup department, and you need money."

Ilana perked up a little. "Yeah?"

I did some quick math in my head.

"If you stop ruining my show," I said, "*and* do our makeup for dress rehearsal and opening night, I'll pay you five hundred dollars."

"Eep!" Ilana clapped a hand to her mouth to stifle a scream.

"But you have to *really* do a good job," I said.

Without warning, Ilana threw her arms around me and squeezed.

"Thank you, Sunny! I'm so sorry!" She pulled back, and tears were spilling down her cheeks. "And I'm going to make you guys look like superstars, I promise!"

"Good," I said with a genuine smile. Finally, I seemed to be making progress.

But over the course of the week, new worries started to creep into my mind.

If it wasn't bad enough that I'd blown my budget on makeup and that my actors might drop trou in their hand-stapled costumes, there were still no special effects for the show.

Unless I could find a human-sized hamster ball, I wouldn't be dropping from the sky in a bubble, and for the winged monkeys to fly, I'd need million-dollar jetpacks. A bit difficult to come by with a budget of pocket lint.

A week before dress rehearsal, I asked Mom to supervise the cast while I put my artistic talent to work creating special effects.

The only problem? I had no artistic talent.

But I did have a list of the special effects I'd need to make a passable theater academy version of *Wicked*.

1. *Flying monkeys!*
2. *Nessarose's wheelchair moves by itself!*
3. *The Oz machine!*
4. *Flying Elphaba!*
5. *Glinda's bubble!*
6. *Green skin for Elphaba!*
7. *Goat horns for Max!*
8. *Green everything for Emerald City!*
9. *Caged lion cub!*

"This'll be easy!" I told myself as I walked to the art room. "I can do anything!"

I started with the flying monkeys. All I really needed was a dozen cutouts that I could string up and swing from the ceiling. Yes, it would look tacky, but it might distract people from Suresh mouthing his lines while cheap karaoke music played along.

"This'll be easy!" I said again as I printed out a side profile of a monkey from the Internet. "I can do anything!"

I traced the image onto white paper and cut it out, taping a jagged wing to its back. I held it up to survey the completed work.

My flying monkey looked like a flaming squirrel taking a poop.

With a frustrated sigh, I crumpled it and tried again. This time I simply cut out the picture from the printout and taped on a wing.

"Not bad!" I said, punching a hole in the monkey's head.

I laced a piece of string through and held the final product in the air, pulling the string from side to side. Instead of fluttering gracefully, the thin paper flapped and flipped so the monkey seemed to be spiraling out of control.

"Oh, come *on*," I said in exasperation. "Fly already!"

Thinking it might be more like a kite, I gave a running start so a breeze could carry it into the air. Unfortunately, I was so focused on the monkey, I didn't notice the storage rack of paper in my path until I smashed into it face-first.

And the rack happened to have built-in cutting teeth.

"Ow, ow, ow," I whimpered, bringing my hand to my cheek. I pulled it away, and saw a *lot* of blood.

The monkey cutout slipped from my fingers, and I dropped to the floor, clutching my slashed face. The door clicked open, and to add more insult to my injury, Ammo stepped through the door.

"This room is off-limits to theater geeks," he snarled. "What are *you* doing in here?"

There was no fight left in me.

"Bleeding to death on your floor," I whispered. "I ran into the paper holder."

"What?" The sneer on his face disappeared, and he walked over. "Let me see."

I blinked up at him. "Why? So you can rub your thumb in it?"

"Shut up." He took my hand away from my face.

"Careful, it's shockingly gruesome!" I warned.

Ammo's eyebrows pushed together as he studied my cheek, and after a second he got up.

"The blood makes it look worse than it is," he said. "You just need alcohol and a Band-Aid."

I glanced around and picked up the monkey cutout. "How about spit and some paper?"

Ammo actually laughed. "You could do that. Or I have a first aid kit."

He grabbed it out of a cupboard and popped it open.

"Why do you have one of those?" I asked.

"In case strange girls run headfirst into the paper holder," he said, grabbing a swab of rubbing alcohol and a Band-Aid. "A better question is . . . why did you do that?"

In answer, I held up the monkey cutout.

"It won't fly," I said pitifully.

Ammo just stared. "It's a piece of paper. Of course it won't fly."

"It's a *monkey*!" I yelled.

Ammo's eyes widened. "Fine, it's a monkey. But those don't fly either. Hold still." He cupped my chin in one hand and swabbed the alcohol across my cheek.

I jammed my eyes shut and held back a scream as the alcohol seared my skin.

"Almost done," he said, applying the Band-Aid. "There."

"Thank you," I said, cradling my cheek. "And I *know* monkeys don't fly. But I have to make a dozen of them do it anyway." I thrust my to-do list in his face. "And then I have to paint a town green and a person green and break into the zoo and steal a lion cub!"

My rant was wasted on Ammo. He'd stopped listening and was smoothing out my crumpled cutout. "This is way too small."

I glowered at him as I wiped the blood off my hands. "The monkey isn't to scale, genius. It's from a picture."

He raised an eyebrow at me. "Actually, *genius*, I meant it's too small to see from the audience." He walked away, holding the wrinkled cutout in the air. "Tell me when it stops looking like a monkey."

"It *never* looked like a monkey," I said miserably.

But I knew what he meant. The farther away he got, the more it became just a shapeless blob. He crumpled it up and threw it in the garbage.

"You need to draw it bigger," he said. "Like . . . ten times bigger. And mount it on cardboard."

I goggled at him. "That's insane. First, I don't know how to draw a monkey. Second, it'll take way too much paper. Third, once they're on cardboard, they'll be giant safety hazards dangling above people's heads."

Ammo frowned, and it struck me that the meanest kid in school was trying to help.

"Sorry," I said. "But—"

"Shadow puppets," he said. "Make shadow puppets."

I gave him a strange look but lifted my hands and tried to form them into a flying monkey shape.

Ammo rolled his eyes. "Not with your *hands*. With paper!"

I pointed at the garbage can. "Help yourself to my latest masterpiece."

"I'm talking about shadow plays." Ammo sat in front of the computer and did a quick search. "In China people make these elaborate cutout puppets and move them in front of a lamp. People in the audience can see the shadows against a backdrop."

He scooted sideways so I could see the images.

My eyebrows rose. "Wow. Those are amazing!" I said. Then I looked at Ammo. "How do you know about art from China?"

"I'm an artist," he said. "Thanks for noticing."

I frowned. "I've noticed. Remember your fancy place cards with the mean things written on them?"

Ammo turned back to the computer. "You had it coming for being a snob."

I gasped in indignation. "I had it coming?! I'm not the one who started this. You've been picking on us since I cast your brother . . . oh, my God." I trailed off. "Please don't tell me that's what this is all about."

Ammo hammered on the keyboard with his fingers. "We do everything together. I didn't think he'd take this theater crap so seriously."

"Fine, I get that," I said. "But you didn't have to call

people names. Or draw mean pictures." I cleared my throat. "Or make slant eyes at them."

There was nothing from Ammo but silence. He stared at the computer screen, unmoving. The only thing that blinked was the cursor.

"I didn't mean it as a race thing," he finally said. "It was just an easy way to make fun of you." He turned toward me. "I don't have a problem with Asians. Personally, I love fried rice."

A smile accidentally formed on my lips. "I'm glad. But there's nothing wrong with the other kids either."

He shrugged. "I don't know . . . that kid with the big eyes creeps me out."

"Tim's harmless," I said. "He actually adopted a whole bunch of kittens and . . ." I gasped and clapped my hands together.

Ammo watched me in alarm. "What? He's going to eat them?"

"No, I just had a brilliant idea!" I exclaimed. "I'll borrow one of Tim's kittens for the lion cub!"

I reached for my to-do list and scribbled a note. "One task down!" I cheered. "And if I can get the shadow puppet thing to work, that's another one!"

Ammo glanced at the list. "Make that three. If you

put a green lens over the spotlight, it'll turn everything on stage green, and you'll have your Emerald City."

I almost snapped my pencil in two, writing like mad. "*You* are a *genius*! Now, that green lens thingy: Can I buy one for free?"

Again, Ammo was ignoring me, staring intently at the list. "You know, you can move the wheelchair by tying heavy-duty fishing line to it and pulling it from offstage."

"Oh! Good one!" I started to write, but Ammo grabbed the list from me and paced the room, chewing his bottom lip.

"The bubble, though, that's tricky," he said.

"Especially since I have to float down from the ceiling," I said.

Ammo shook his head. "Won't work. You're too heavy."

"Hey!" I frowned at him.

He rolled his eyes. "You're too heavy for what I'm thinking," he corrected. "A papier-mâché half bubble."

"Oh," I said. "Why not a whole bubble?"

Ammo flipped to a clean page in my notebook and started sketching. "Because a half bubble will give the illusion that you're *in* a bubble but people will still be able to see you." He shaded a few spots and held up his finished work.

The sketch was of a female figure standing in the center of a half dome, her hands clutching the curved sides while her feet poked out of the bottom.

"That looks like something Lady Gaga would wear," I said.

"You have to use your imagination," said Ammo. "A little fog on the ground while you glide forward with the bubble around you . . ."

I tilted my head to one side and squinted at the image. "Maybe."

"Trust me," said Ammo. "It'll work."

"Okay. So . . . how do I get started?" I eyed the clock on the wall. "And how long is this going to take? I've got lines to practice."

"Go," he said, shooing me away with a hand. "The frame comes first anyway."

I took a step and hesitated. "Are . . . are you sure? I can take care of this."

He raised an eyebrow at me. "Do you even know how to *make* papier-mâché?"

"Easy. You get some strips of paper," I said.

"And?"

I thought. "And . . . a . . . machete."

"Not even close," said Ammo. "Look, this is *my* area

of expertise. Why don't you let me handle it?"

"Fine," I said, crossing my arms.

I wanted him to know I was giving up begrudgingly, but the funny thing was, the moment I did, I actually felt freer. Like Ammo had literally taken a burden off my shoulders.

"You know what?" I said with a smile. "I think I *will* leave this up to you. Thanks, Ammo."

"Kyle," he mumbled, head down as he worked on another sketch. "My name's Kyle."

I nodded at him. "Kyle. Thank you."

He glanced up. "You're welcome."

Knowing I was long overdue for a scene, I hurried from the room, almost colliding with Derek as he headed toward me.

"Hey, I was coming to see if you needed help," he said.

"Actually, *Kyle* could use your help in the art room," I said.

Derek didn't move. "Kyle who?"

I couldn't help feeling a little smug as I said, "Your brother. I'm going to make him the art director."

EIGHTEEN

ONCE I STARTED HOARDING POWER less and distributing it more, it was amazing how things came together. Over the week, Kyle had the Melodramatics work on special effects when they weren't in a scene. They draped papier-mâche over a wire frame to make my half bubble, and they cut out monkeys that Kyle had drawn to make shadow puppets.

Tim agreed to let me use Fig Mewton in the show as long as I included him in the playbill. Ilana found a recipe to make *safe* green face paint for Anne Marie, and Max's mom even agreed to hem costumes after he accidentally mooned a school bus in his trousers.

With all of us pitching in, we had singing, dancing, scenery, makeup, and costumes under wraps.

The only thing we didn't have was an audience. I decided to tell everyone why, and shared what Cam had told me about separate ticket sales.

"We really need to promote our show," I told the Melodramatics the week we started blocking.

"I can get my parents to come," said Anne Marie.

"We can *all* get our parents to come," I said. "But we need people who didn't change our diapers to show up. Spread the word!"

The Monday after that, Bree and I swung by the front office to see how ticket sales had been.

"You've sold fifty," said the cashier.

I sighed. "That would be everyone's parents."

"And siblings," said Bree. "How many people does the theater seat?"

"Two hundred," I said.

We walked out of the office and headed for the auditorium.

"I don't get it," I said. "People love *Wicked*. Why wouldn't they want to see it?"

"No offense to us," she said, "but look at the two casts. *Wicked* is full of no-names; *Mary Pops In* is full of *known* names. People are going to see kids they recognize. And they don't know if we have any talent."

I pointed at her and smiled triumphantly. "Then we have to show them. What do they always play before a movie?"

Bree made a face. "Commercials."

"No, not commercials!" I rapped on her skull with my knuckles. "Previews! Trailers for upcoming films to get you interested in them."

She gave me a dubious look. "You want to make a trailer for our show."

"Why not?" I asked. "We can borrow an AV camera, film at today's practice and air it for the next two weeks during morning announcements."

I tugged her in the direction of the AV equipment room.

"How do we decide what to put in the trailer?" she asked.

"We'll use little clips of us singing, a couple of brief words. Trust me. It'll be great," I said.

I signed out one of the cameras and turned on the power.

"Bree Hill," I aimed it at her, "tell me something wicked!"

"That's a cute idea!" She laughed and rubbed her chin.

"Wicked . . . wicked. Oh! I once stole a lipstick from the sample counter at Macy's."

I made a face. "You stole a used lipstick?"

"Yeah. The one you like to borrow," she said with an evil grin.

"Eeew!" I squealed. "*That* is wicked."

She took the camera from me. "What about you, Sunny Kim? What wicked thing have you done?"

I leaned in. "I accidentally dropped my dad's toothbrush in the toilet and put it back before he found out."

"Ugh!" Bree laughed, and we ran into Blakely with the camera.

We told the other kids our idea to boost ticket sales, and they were beyond excited. I started pulling people aside for wicked confessions, most of which turned out to be pretty funny.

"I once hid Kyle's goldfish and told him we were having them for dinner," said Derek. "Then I asked my mom to cook fish sticks."

Kyle punched him in the arm. "That's okay. Because I wrapped an Axe label around a glue stick and told Derek it was a pocket-size deodorant."

After I'd gotten all my confessions, I taped bits of the show and had someone else handle the scenes I was in.

"Who are you going to get to make the final trailer?" asked Derek at the end of practice. "Because Kyle and I are pretty good at that kind of stuff. We could work together on something."

Kyle grinned at Derek.

"That would be awesome," I said. I checked my watch and smiled apologetically. "Sorry, but I have to make a phone call."

I told everyone good-bye and slipped into an empty classroom to call Stefan. This time, instead of animals or violins, I heard a voice through a loudspeaker, followed by cheering in the background.

"Hey, Sunny!" Stefan yelled into the phone.

"Where are you now?" I asked.

"Method acting!" he told me. "Me and the other guys are finished getting ready for your special favor for Chase. We're just making sure we have everything right."

"You're finished?" I asked, pumping my fist in the air. "Can you guys meet me this Wednesday?"

"Of course!" he said. "Just give me the address."

I told him and hurried back to the theater to wait for Chase's group to arrive. Ilana was one of the first, and she eyed me suspiciously.

"Hey," I told her. "Just waiting for Chase."

She nodded. "I think he's arguing with his dad again."

I frowned. "He still won't come to the show, huh?"

"Not even if Chase ends it by diving into a cup of water," said Ilana.

Chase walked over, his forehead wrinkling in confusion. "Hey . . . guys," he said. "What's going on?"

"Ilana and I just had a big catfight," I said. "You missed it."

Ilana nodded. "But we'll be at it again tomorrow for an encore." She waved at me and walked away.

"Okay," Chase said with a laugh. He shoved his hands in his pockets. "I'm glad you two are getting along again." He bumped my shoulder with his, and I giggled.

Why did that happen *every* time he came in contact with me?

"And I'm glad you made up with the rest of your cast," he said.

"With *your* help," I said, nudging him back.

He let out a high-pitched giggle that mirrored mine.

"Stop it!" I said with a laugh.

"So, why *are* you here?" he asked.

"I couldn't remember if you were busy on Wednesday," I said. "Are you?"

"Yeah. Baseball game." Chase made a face. "I'd skip it, but my dad's going to be in the stands."

"Perfect!" I said enthusiastically.

Judging by the weird look on Chase's face, I must have said it *too* enthusiastically.

"Uh . . . because I want to watch you play!" I said.

Chase's face brightened. "Really?"

In reality I only wanted to see the first few minutes, but he seemed so happy. How could I say no?

"Sure!" I said. "Gooo, baseball!"

I punched my fist in the air, which looked even stupider than I'd predicted, but Chase didn't seem to mind.

He grinned. "Great! So, Wednesday night. At the ball field."

"Tell your dad to save me a seat," I said.

"Sure," he said.

I should have told Chase to save the seat in front of Mr. O'Malley as well . . . to hold his jaw when it dropped.

Wednesday night, Bree and Suresh followed me into the stands at the baseball game.

"Are you sure this is a good idea?" Suresh asked. "Chase's dad might just get really angry."

“This’ll work,” I told him. “Trust me.”

“Last time you said that, Anne Marie’s face looked like a giant pea,” said Bree.

“Yeah, well, this time’s going to be different,” I said.

I glanced into the stands and saw Mr. O’Malley sitting by himself.

“Come on,” I said. “And act cool.”

“I’m Indian,” said Suresh with a sniff. “Cool is in my DNA.”

We made our way up the steps to Mr. O’Malley’s row, and I waved to him.

“Sunny!” he said, patting the seat beside him. “Good to see you!”

“Thanks, Mr. O’Malley.” I gestured to Bree and Suresh. “These are my friends. They’re in the *Wicked* show with me.”

Mr. O’Malley shook their hands. “I’m impressed with you kids, taking on your own show. How’s it going?”

“If we can sell one hundred fifty tickets in the next week, it’ll be great,” I said with a tight smile.

He winced. “Sales not so hot?”

“We’re lucky our parents are showing up,” I said. Then I had an idea. “I don’t suppose you’d come to Chase’s *and* ours?”

If I acted like it was a given he'd attend, maybe Mr. O'Malley would feel obligated to go.

"I'm sorry, Sunny," he said with a smooth smile. "But I have an important meeting that evening. I won't even be able to attend Chase's show."

So much for that plan.

Out of the corner of my eye, I saw movement on the field. Stefan, wearing a baseball uniform and cleats, was pushing a sound system in front of the stands. I straightened in my seat.

"Looks like they're getting started," I said.

A bunch of guys in uniform walked out onto the field, followed by a girl. Chase, who was standing on the pitcher's mound, watched in confusion. So did his father.

"What on earth?" mumbled Mr. O'Malley.

Stefan switched on the sound, and the girl's voice carried into the stands.

"Shoeless Joe from Hannibal, MO! That's my story, fellas! And I got a feeling it's only the beginning!"

The crowd buzzed as a musical intro played.

Mr. O'Malley's jaw dropped. "This is a musical number!"

Everyone else in the stands realized it as well and started cheering. The girl and the guys in baseball uniforms sang and danced around Chase, who stood rooted to the spot, swiveling his head to follow them. Meanwhile, the crowd clapped their hands to the rhythm . . . except Mr. O'Malley. He was frowning and rubbing his forehead.

I glanced at Bree and Suresh, who gave me an *I told you so* look. I turned back to Mr. O'Malley and cautiously tapped his arm.

"Sir? Is . . . is something wrong?" I shouted above the rhythmic clapping of the crowd.

He gestured down onto the field. "Chase *knows* this number. He did it for an elementary talent show."

"Awww," I said, smiling. "That's nice."

"Not when I know he's better than the rest of them, but he's just standing there!"

A smile spread slowly across my face, and it was all I could do to keep from hugging Mr. O'Malley. Bree and Suresh grinned at me and exchanged a subtle high-five with each other. I nudged Bree and stood in my seat.

"Chase! Chase! Chase! Chase!" I hollered in time to the music.

Bree and Suresh hopped up and joined the cry.

"Chase! Chase! Chase! Chase!"

People around us started shouting too, and soon even Mr. O'Malley was clapping and mumbling under his breath.

Chase finally heard his name over the music and turned

around. At first he stared at *me*, wide-eyed and embarrassed, but then his eyes traveled to his dad. The expression on Chase's face was priceless. His forehead wrinkled in confusion, and his nostrils flared with emotion.

"*Dance*!" I yelled, gesturing to the rest of the team.

Chase shook himself out of his stupor and jumped into line with the rest of the ball players, quickly catching up to their foot movements. When Chase picked the girl up and twirled her behind his back, Mr. O'Malley actually *whooped*.

The dance number ended much too soon, and the audience gave them a standing ovation. Stefan emerged from the group and stood facing the stands.

"If you enjoyed that number," he said breathlessly, "the Carnegie Arts Academy is putting on *two* musicals next weekend, *Wicked* and *Mary Pops In*. I recommend them both."

If I'd had any budget money left, I would have thrown it gratefully at his feet.

"Ooh, *Wicked*," said a woman sitting in front of me. "I love that show."

Mr. O'Malley leaned forward and tapped her on the shoulder. When she turned, he said, "Some of the stars are right here." He pointed to me, Suresh, and Bree.

The three of us blushed and waved.

"*Really?*" said the woman.

"This one sings like a bird," said Mr. O'Malley, pointing at me. "You should check out the show."

I smiled and ducked my head. "Thank you, sir!"

"Hey, O'Malley!" a guy called to him. "Was that your kid out there?"

My body tensed, and I gave Chase's dad a worried look. Would this ruin it? Would he be embarrassed?

Mr. O'Malley turned a little red but said, "Yep, that's my Chase!"

"Strong kid!" the guy called back.

I melted into a puddle in my seat.

The game started, and I had to admit, it wasn't bad. Chase struck out batter after batter, and his team went on to win the game by four runs. When it ended and everyone was clearing the stands, Chase came up to greet us.

"Hey!" He hugged me and Bree and bumped fists with Suresh. "I'm glad you guys came." It took him a second longer to look at Mr. O'Malley. "Hey, Dad."

"Chase." Mr. O'Malley clapped a hand on his shoulder. "Very impressive out there."

Chase grinned and rotated his pitching shoulder. "I've been working on my curveball."

His dad's face turned solemn. "I meant all of it, son."

Bree and Suresh motioned to me and tiptoed away. I moved to follow them, but Chase's fingers caught my wrist, and he cast me a pleading glance. I froze and did my best not to listen in on the conversation.

"You're impressed by all of what?" Chase asked. I could tell he wasn't daring to hope. "The baseball?"

I tried to make myself as invisible as possible, which was hard to do with Chase holding my wrist in a death grip.

"I'm just gonna sit and let you two talk," I whispered, trying to break free.

Thankfully, Chase let go of my wrist, but his hand traveled down to mine and clenched that instead.

"No, son," said his dad, clearing his throat. "You did pretty well with the musical stuff, too."

Chase smashed my fingers in his, and I pressed my lips together to suppress a scream.

"Seriously? I didn't even practice that," he said with a tentative smile. "But I *have* been working like crazy on *Mary Pops In*." He paused. "That's pretty responsible."

Mr. O'Malley was quiet for so long, I almost forgot about the pain in my hand.

"It is," he told Chase, offering his own tentative smile. "And I'll bet it looks great."

"We're almost sold out of seats for the show," Chase ventured, "but I could still get you one."

Chase squeezed my hand so tightly, I felt my knuckles rubbing against each other.

"Please, Mr. O'Malley!" I finally squeaked. "Go to the show so I can have my hand back!"

Mr. O'Malley chuckled, and Chase gave a start, as if he'd forgotten he was crushing me and not a soda can. He let go of my hand, and I collapsed in a seat.

"Sorry," Chase said with a rueful grin. "I keep doing that."

"It's okay." I glanced up at Mr. O'Malley. "Will you please go to his show?"

I watched the two of them stare at each other, their eyes doing all the talking. As if an unspoken agreement had been reached, Mr. O'Malley took some money out of his wallet and handed Chase two ten-dollar bills.

Chase took it and smiled. "Tickets are only ten bucks."

Mr. O'Malley nodded. "To *your* show. I'd like to go to Sunny's, too."

"I'll take that!" I snatched one of the tens from Chase and beamed at Mr. O'Malley. "Thank you again, sir!"

Mr. O'Malley winked at me and slapped his son on the back. "I'll see you down at the car in a few minutes."

We watched him make his way out of the stands, stopping occasionally to chat with someone. When he'd disappeared from sight, I pinched Chase's arm.

"Tickets are only ten bucks!" I mimicked.

Chase grinned and gingerly took my hand, pulling me to my feet.

"I'm guessing that stunt before the game was *your* idea," he said.

"Why, yes." I polished my fingernails on my shirtfront. "It was."

He shook his head. "How did you pull it off?"

I put my index finger on the side of Chase's chin and turned his head so he could see Stefan. My acting coach/STARS counselor/dance instructor was busy hustling the audio equipment into a van.

"Remember that little baseball musical the high school did last spring?" I asked. "If you pay them enough, they'll come back and perform a song from it."

Chase gaped at me. "Sunny, you did *not* pay for this."

"Not a *lot*," I said. "Just . . . consider it repayment for all those Chocolate Monkey muffins."

He shook his head. "That's still not enough."

"Of course it is," I said. "You're my best friend and the greatest guy I know. If I could afford it, I would have had the original cast out there." I pointed to the field. "It would have been incredibly moving."

Chase smiled. "I think most of the original cast is dead."

"Then it would have been incredibly creepy," I said.

He laughed and squeezed my hand. "Well, let me at least *try* to repay you," he said.

"How?" I asked.

Without another word, Chase leaned in and pressed his lips against mine. I closed my eyes and kissed him back. After a few seconds, he pulled away, grinning sheepishly.

"So?" he asked.

I tilted my hand from side to side. "That was *maybe* a nickel's worth of payment."

Chase's jaw dropped. "*That* was totally a quarter! And you kissed me back."

"I was being polite," I said, wrapping my arms around his neck. "I'll need a lot more of those to make us even."

Chase grinned. "Then I've got a million for you."

NINETEEN

ON THE MORNING OF THE big showcase, everyone in the Melodramatics was incredibly tense. In any part of the school where one of us was present, the conversation had a common theme—stage diva.

In the cafeteria: "I asked for tea with lemon, not lime! How is a taste of the tropics going to help my singing voice?"

In the bathroom: "Use that hairspray somewhere else. It could crystallize in my throat!"

In the hallway: "Don't step on my toes! Do you *want* me to fall over when I dance?"

And that was just me.

By the time I gathered the others for a lunchtime pump-up, everyone looked ready to claw the nearest throat. At one point Derek bent down to tie his shoe and accidentally bumped into Suresh.

"Watch it, dude!" Suresh snapped.

"Give me room!" Derek snapped back.

"I'll give you my foot up—"

"Guys!" I said, walking around the group. "Let's all take a minute to relax and breathe."

I closed my eyes and led by example, slowly inhaling and exhaling. Around me, I could hear several people doing the same.

I could also hear, "Don't breathe so close to me. I don't want your germs."

"You've been fine with Janice spitting on you all this time!"

"Hey, I have my braces off now!"

I opened my eyes. "Okay, there's pre-show nerves and then there's *this*." I looked from person to person. "*What* is going on?"

Nobody answered, and several people suddenly found the carpet very fascinating.

"I know what'll make you feel better," I said. "I was going to save this until later, but . . . we've sold a hundred and fifty seats! Yaaay!" I clapped, but nobody joined in. Not even Holly.

Finally, Cole stepped forward. "I-I'm worried about tonight," he said.

"Why?" I asked.

"I-I'm stuttering a-again," he said. "Nnnow that I knnnow all the lines, i-it's back."

"Have you tried focusing on what you want to say first?" suggested Wendy.

Cole shook his head. "That . . . that's not the problem. I-I knnnow what I . . . what I . . . want to say."

I chewed my lip. "It's just stuck," I said.

Cole nodded.

Bree nudged me. "Can't we fix this like we did Suresh's singing? Just record someone reading Cole's lines?"

I shook my head. "We don't have time for him to practice lip-synching."

"It's not just Cole," Holly spoke up.

Everyone turned to look at her.

"I'm worried too," she said in a small voice. "I've never been onstage for so long. And with a hundred fifty people staring at me?" She shuddered. "What if I make a mistake?"

"The *Mary Pops In* cast is, like, perfect," agreed Anne Marie. "And we're . . . *not*."

"We're doomed," said Tim.

Several people voiced their agreement until I quieted them with a shout.

"You know what?" I said, climbing onto the stage. "It doesn't matter if we're not perfect. In real life, *nobody* is." I pointed at Cole. "You have a stutter. Real people have stutters. You're going onstage and that's final."

"But—"

I silenced him with a hand. "Don't you guys remember why we're doing this? To prove that there's nothing wrong with us the way we are!"

Suresh cleared his throat. "Does that mean I can sing my own songs?"

I looked at him. "No."

"But a bad singer is who I are!" he said.

Everyone laughed.

"I'm not talking about talent, guys," I said, grinning. "I'm talking about the little differences that get us branded as rejects or weirdos. Whether it's being overweight or having a stutter or even being from a different culture."

Several people nodded.

I tapped the side of my head. "We're smarter than the *Mary Pops In* cast. People may think they're perfect . . . *I* once thought they were perfect . . . but that means their show has to be perfect too."

"Which no show ever is," added Bree.

"Exactly!" I said. "We're not the perfect cast trying to put on the perfect show. People know little hiccups are going to happen."

I sat on the edge of the stage and grabbed Holly's arm. "You can make mistakes, and people are still going to love you because you have that energy," I said. "And the longer you're up there, the more in love they'll be."

Holly's face broke into a cautious grin. "Really?"

"Really," I said with a smile.

Bree glanced around at the other Melodramatics. "Guys, we go onstage in six hours!" she said. "Aren't you excited?"

"Yeah," a couple people said, while the others nodded.

I cupped a hand around my ear. "What?"

"Yeah!" This time everyone responded. Holly even gave a little bounce.

I jumped down from the stage.

"What?!" I hollered.

"Yeah!!" everyone shouted.

I held my hand out, palm down, and smiled at Cole. He

smiled back and put his hand on top of mine. Bree added hers, then Suresh, and soon there was a giggling and slapping of hands as everyone joined the center.

"'*Wicked* kids rule' on three!" shouted Max. "One, two, three!"

The cheer of the Melodramatics practically shook the walls of the theater.

"*WICKED* KIDS RULE!"

As the hours ticked by before the performance, I rushed from place to place, making sure everything was ready for a seven o'clock curtain call.

"Are costumes ready behind the stage exits for quick changes?" I asked Cole, who I'd put in charge of wardrobe. "I need to get from my Glinda gown into my Shiz school outfit in seconds."

He nodded. "W-wear the Shiz o-outfit under your gown," he said.

I snapped my fingers. "Good idea!" I turned to Max, who I'd put in charge of curtains. "Did you make sure the ropes work in case the electric panel shorts out?"

He nodded. "I even brought gloves so I can pull the ropes fast."

"Clever!" I said. I turned to Kyle, who was busy making

last-minute adjustments to my bubble. "Do you have the monkeys and the green light lens and the fishing line and—"

Kyle turned to scowl at me.

"Good job," I said, patting his shoulder.

"Hey, Sunny?" Bree beckoned me backstage, a huge smile on her face.

"What's up?" I asked.

She pointed to the loading dock door, which someone had opened for a trio of vans. Standing beside the vans was a crowd of men and women in suits and skirts. Some were carrying musical instruments, and all were gazing at a man who was giving instructions.

"Dad?!" I cried.

He stopped midsentence and gestured at me.

"Everyone, this is my daughter, Sunny, the show's director and star. Sunny, this is your orchestra."

The men and women clapped politely. I just gawked at them until Bree nudged me, and I finally smiled and waved.

"Oh . . . my . . . God," I whispered to Bree.

"I know!" she whispered back.

"So, as I was saying," Dad said, returning his attention to the orchestra, "this is an abbreviated version of the full show. Don't be surprised when you skip multiple songs." He rubbed his hands together. "That's it, and thank you again for coming."

Another man, I guessed the conductor by his fancy clothes, motioned the members into the theater, smiling to me as he passed. A xylophone and a harp rolled by, followed by two trumpeters. I stared at them and then at Dad.

"So?" he asked, holding his arms open. "What do you think?"

"Dad!" I ran into his arms and squeezed him tight. "How did you do this?"

"I worked on a sound track for a friend of mine last year," he said, "and he owed me a favor." Dad bent down and whispered, "You're also good practice for the conductor. He's from the *Wicked* roadshow coming to town."

I gasped and clutched at Dad's arm. "Are you serious? That's perfect!"

Dad grinned. "That's why I thought you wouldn't mind."

"Thank you, thank you, thank you!" I hugged him again, then turned and hugged Bree. "Isn't this awesome?" I asked.

"Yes!" she said. "But we have to get into costume!"

I checked my watch. "Oh, crap. We do!" I gave Dad a

kiss on the cheek and grabbed Bree's hand. "See you later!" I called to Dad.

"Break a leg out there!" he called back.

The dressing room was a nightmare, packed with girls struggling into dresses and curling their hair.

"Where's Anne Marie?" I asked, spinning in my gown to find her and almost knocking Janice off her feet.

"She's with Ilana getting her makeup done," said Janice.

I nodded. "When you're finished, start gathering people for the circle."

There was a knock on the dressing room door, followed by screams from some of the partially clothed girls. I shifted my huge dress past chairs and people to open it a crack.

"Sunny!" Stefan's face beamed from the other side.

"Hi!" I slipped into the hallway and reached out to hug him, but he held a single rose between us.

My first theater flower.

"That's so sweet!" I gushed.

Stefan smirked. "I would have given you more, but I didn't want to upstage someone." He shifted aside, and Chase stepped forward holding a bouquet.

I squealed and took the flowers before giving him a huge hug.

"Easy there," said Stefan, tugging me back. "I have someone I want you to meet." He grabbed me by the hand and led me toward the audience. "By the way, kudos on the orchestra," he said in a low voice. "Your show is quite the hit already."

"Really?" I asked, giggling.

Now that I was down on the floor, the audience could see me in my gown, and they whispered excitedly.

I felt giddy and lightheaded and on top of the world. *Now* I knew why people fought so hard to be a part of theater.

Stefan walked up to a mustached man seated front and center. He stood when we drew closer and smiled.

"Sunny," said Stefan, "this is Marcus Kramer, director of the STARS program. Mr. Kramer, this is the actress/director extraordinaire I've been telling you about." He grinned at me.

Mr. Kramer extended his hand, and I almost tripped over the woman sitting beside him trying to reach it.

"*So* nice to meet you, sir," I said.

"The privilege is all mine," he said. "Stefan's been filling me in on how this performance came to be, and I understand you were instrumental in it."

I bit my lip shyly. "We all were, sir," I said. "Even him." I nodded to Stefan.

Mr. Kramer chuckled. "That's very humble of you. I look forward to watching you act, especially since we have a last-minute opening to fill."

"Really?" My heart skipped a beat . . . but then his words sank in, and I frowned. "Is it because of Ilana Rourke, sir?"

Mr. Kramer started in surprise. "Why . . . yes. As you know, we only accept quality applicants."

My forehead wrinkled. What did quality have to do with Ilana not having money? "Sorry, sir?"

"Apparently, she was only an understudy for the role she's playing tonight," said Stefan. "She lucked into this part."

Wow.

Three weeks ago, I would have laughed and done my best to impress Mr. Kramer. But now . . .

"Sir, I think there's been a misunderstanding," I said. "Ilana is a *great* actress. And she didn't even try for the starring role this year because . . ." I squeezed my hands together, hoping one last lie wouldn't kill me. "Because she wanted to share the theater experience and not hog the spotlight."

Stefan gave me a look, but Mr. Kramer raised an eyebrow. "That's very admirable."

I nodded. "She'd be an asset to your program, sir. I think you should keep her."

Stefan rubbed his temple and stared daggers at me. I knew what he was thinking . . . I'd just blown a chance at STARS.

"Well, thank you for that honest insight, Ms. Kim," said Mr. Kramer.

I smiled politely. "You're welcome. Excuse me, I have a show to start." With an apologetic look at Stefan, I gathered my dress and turned away.

"Not so fast," Mom's voice sounded from over my shoulder.

I spun around and practically tripped over the poor woman next to Mr. Kramer again. Mom and Grandma had been sitting two seats away, and I hadn't even noticed!

"You should meet the agent I was telling you about," said Mom. She gestured to the woman beside Mr. Kramer.

Of course.

"Sorry!" In my flustered state, I attempted to curtsy. "How do you do. Sunny Kim."

"Evelyn Kramer," she said, offering me her hand.

I took it and hesitated in confusion. "Kramer?"

Mr. Kramer leaned over. "My wife. Show business is a small world," he said with a wink.

I laughed and curtsied again, being sure to give Mrs. Kramer her hand back. "Well, it's very nice to meet you.

And if you'll excuse me, there are people on*stage* waiting for me to trip over them, too."

Everyone laughed, and Mr. Kramer put a hand on my arm.

"Ms. Kim, we're also looking for talented directors," he said. "If you know any . . ." He let the comment hang in the air.

I smiled shyly. "We'll see."

As I walked off, I heard him tell Stefan, "Yes, we will."

The rest of the cast were already waiting in a circle when I finally made it backstage.

"Everybody ready?" I asked.

"To throw up?" asked Suresh. "Yes."

"We're going to be fine," I said.

I stepped between Bree and Derek and grabbed their hands. Everyone else followed suit. I could almost feel the floor shaking with our nervous energy.

"Remember," I said. "We're all average people. Except for those two." I pointed to Anne Marie's green face and Max's goat horns.

We all laughed.

"Do your best, and I'll be so proud," I said. "Let's bow our heads."

Every head went down and I said a quick prayer. When

it was over, I squeezed Bree and Derek's hands and stepped out of the circle.

"Places, please," I said. "It's almost showtime."

Kyle approached with a head mic and I clipped it over my ear. While everyone else moved into position, I slipped through the curtain and walked to center stage. There was a loud click from overhead, followed by a blinding spotlight, and I blinked to adjust my eyes.

A sea of faces stared back at me. Even though I'd seen most of them before, they were way more intimidating when I was in a ballgown and not a potato sack.

"Hello," I said to the crowd.

"Hi, pretty lady!" a child's voice shrieked from somewhere near the back.

Everyone in the audience laughed, and so did I.

"Nice. Can I take you with me everywhere?" I asked the unseen child.

The audience laughed again.

"My name is Sunny Kim," I said. "And I'm Galinda, the future Good Witch of the North."

From all around me speakers crackled and boomed. At first I thought it was *my* microphone until a voice that wasn't mine spoke.

"She's also our director," the voice said. It sounded suspiciously like Suresh.

I giggled nervously and shrugged at the audience. "Well—"

There was a scuffling sound over the speakers.

"And she took a chance on us when nobody else would!" Max shouted into the mic, even though I could hear him plainly without it.

"Dude!" said Suresh's voice. "Stop stealing my thunder."

"Please," said Max. "Like you're not gonna get enough attention in those tight pants."

I sighed and stared at the ceiling, but the audience just laughed.

There was another scuffling sound, followed by a whispery voice.

"Let her finish so we can start the show!" Bree's voice came from above.

"Thank you!" I shouted over my shoulder. I turned back to the audience with a broad smile. "Anyway, this first show is about appreciating the differences in everyone."

My eyes scanned the audience and stopped on a certain face in the crowd . . . Grandma's. She smiled, and I felt emotion tug at my throat. "Some of them you don't see as gifts at first," I said, glancing to the stage exit where Kyle was watching, "but if you add a little spit and polish, you really see them shine."

I paused and held up a finger. "And for the record, I didn't actually spit on anyone."

The audience laughed again, and it sounded so wonderful echoing off the walls. There was much more I wanted to say, about the struggles we'd gone through and the fears we were fighting just to be on that stage.

But the story wasn't all mine to tell. Behind the heavy velvet curtain waited a crowd of talented and underappreciated actors, eager to share their voices.

It was time to let them speak.

"Ladies and gentlemen," I said, the curtain creeping open behind me, "the Melodramatics of Carnegie Arts Academy are proud to be . . . *Wicked*."

The orchestra blasted the opening chords over thunderous applause, and I ran offstage to let the show begin.

THE END

Did you **LOVE** this book?

Want to get access to great books for **FREE?**

Join

<u>where you can</u>

✗ Read great books for FREE! ✗

Get exclusive excerpts

≶ Chat with your friends ⩔

◉ Vote on polls ◉

Log on to everloop.com
and join the book loop group!